From *The Black-Headed Pins*

We finished our coffee, and Doris stood up. "Well—don't you be scared, dearie. You just make a dash upstairs to your bedroom, and it'll all be over in a minute."

I thought of Rhynda and immediately convinced myself that she would be back in her bed by this time and that I had better take Doris's advice.

She announced that she was going to leave the kitchen light on, said good night to me, and went off to her room.

I started into the back hall and then realized that the downstairs hall light had either gone out or been switched off.

I backed into the kitchen again, relieved myself by swearing softly but luridly, and controlled a strong desire to cry.

I decided to go around by the butler's pantry, dining room, and the large drawing room, where I could turn on the lights as I went along.

I got through the butler's pantry, and leaving the door wide, found my way easily to the dining-room switch. With the dining room comfortably flooded with light, I started back to turn off the switch in the butler's pantry.

Something odd about the dining-room table caught my attention, and I turned to look. It was the telephone that I had last seen on the bedside table in my old room. I stared at it and then bent down to look at it more closely.

The mouthpiece was stained with blood.

Books by Constance & Gwenyth Little

The Grey Mist Murders (1938)
The Black-Headed Pins (1938)
The Black Gloves (1939)
Black Corridors (1940)
The Black Paw (1941)
The Black Shrouds (1941)
The Black Thumb (1942)
The Black Rustle (1943)
The Black Honeymoon (1944)
Great Black Kanba (1944)
The Black Eye (1945)
The Black Stocking (1946)
The Black Goatee (1947)
The Black Coat (1948)
The Black Piano (1948)
The Black Smith (1950)
The Black House (1950)
The Blackout (1951)
The Black Dream (1952)
The Black Curl (1953)
The Black Iris (1953)

The
Black-Headed Pins
By Constance & Gwenyth Little

The Rue Morgue Press
Boulder, Colorado

The Black-Headed Pins

About the authors

Although all but one of their books had "black" in the title, the 21 mysteries of Constance (1899-1980) and Gwenyth (1903-1985) Little were far from somber affairs. The two Australian-born sisters from East Orange, New Jersey, were far more interested in coaxing chuckles than in inducing chills from their readers.

Indeed, after their first book, *The Grey Mist Murders*, appeared in 1938, Constance rebuked an interviewer for suggesting that their murders weren't realistic by saying, "Our murderers strangle. We have no sliced-up corpses in our books." However, as the books mounted, the Littles did go in for all sorts of gruesome murder methods—"horrible," was the way their own mother described them—which included the occasional sliced-up corpse. But the murders were always off stage and tempered by comic scenes in which bodies and other objects, including swimming pools, were constantly disappearing and reappearing. The action took place in large old mansions, boarding houses, hospitals, hotels, or on trains or ocean liners, anywhere the Littles could gather together a large cast of eccentric characters, many of whom seemed to have escaped from a Kaufman play or a Capra movie. The typical Little heroine—each book was a stand-alone—often fell under suspicion herself and turned detective to keep the police from slapping the cuffs on. Whether she was a working woman or a spoiled little rich brat, she always spoke her mind, kept her sense of humor, and got her man, both murderer and husband. But if marriage was in the offing, it was always on her terms and the vows were taken with more than a touch of cynicism. Love was grand, but it was even grander if the husband could either pitch in with the cooking and cleaning or was wealthy enough to hire household help.

The Littles wrote all their books in bed—"Chairs give one backaches," Gwenyth complained—with Constance providing detailed plot outlines while Gwenyth did the final drafts. Over the years that pattern changed somewhat but Constance always insisted that Gwen "not mess up my clues." Those clues were everywhere and the Littles made sure there were no loose ends. Seemingly irrelevant events were revealed to be of major significance in the final summation.

The Littles published their two final novels, *The Black Curl* and *The Black Iris*, in 1953, and if they missed writing after that, they were at least able to devote more time to their real passion—traveling. The two made at least three trips around the world at a time when that would have been a major expedition. For more information on the Littles and their books, see the introductions by Tom & Enid Schantz to The Rue Morgue Press editions of *The Black Gloves* and *The Black Honeymoon*.

CHAPTER
1

I HATE OLD HOUSES—and I have a special hatred for large old houses. As far as I am concerned, "old-world" and "antique" mean cracks that conceal spiders and roaches, holes that are nothing more than doorways for mice, and insecurely fitted windows that let in just enough wind to sway portieres and drapes. I shall never again live in a house that is not absolutely new, with varnished floors and clean, bright paper on the walls.

I don't think Mrs. Ballinger liked the house either. It was a great rambling barn of a place in the wilds of Sussex County, New Jersey, and had belonged to her husband before he died, but they had never lived in it. Mrs. Ballinger paid taxes on it for a year or two, but nobody would rent or buy it, and at last she couldn't stand it any longer—taxes going out, and nothing coming in—so she moved in herself. The place was filled with dusty, dreary old furniture, and Mrs. Ballinger hired a cook, who had regular days off, and me, as general slave, and set us to work dusting and cleaning up.

She had got me in one of my weak moments. I had recovered from my father's death to find that there simply wasn't any money, and my sister-in-law had come forward and very graciously offered me a home.

Mabel Ballinger was living in the apartment above me at the time, and it wasn't an hour after my sister-in-law had finished being gracious that she came down and offered me a job as companion in her lovely old country place in New Jersey. I accepted thankfully, and by the time I found out that the country place was a dilapidated, creepy old barn, and that Mrs. Ballinger put every penny through a mangle before parting with it, my sister-in-law was miffed and had stopped being gracious.

We moved out to Sussex County in April, and by December I was frantically saving my salary so that I could get a bit ahead and find myself a decent job back in civilization. In the meantime, I took almost fanatical care of the few nice clothes left over from the prosperous days with my father.

Late in the summer, Mrs. Ballinger had decided to ask her nieces and nephews for a Christmas houseparty. It was a mixture of duty and business that had prompted her. She knew she would not see much of them in the winter, and then, one of the nephews, John Ballinger, liked puttering around with tools and always did a great deal of free repair work for her.

One evening a week before Christmas, she sat down in the great drafty old living room with pad and pencil and began solemnly to make out her list of guests.

I sat huddled in an armchair, trying to keep warm and wondering idly whether to waste my breath on a suggestion that we build a wood fire in the fireplace. I knew there were some logs in the cellar, but she had said firmly, at the beginning of the cold weather, that they were to be saved in case something went wrong with the furnace.

I watched her poring over the list and laughed silently. She and I both knew that list by heart. She had no friends of her own age, and she would not have dreamed of wasting money on an outsider in any case. Several times as she sat there she glanced uneasily over her shoulder, not at me, but into the dim corners of the large shadowy room.

After the third time, I said uncomfortably, "Why do you keep looking behind you? Are you—expecting anyone?"

She grew quite irritable. "What on earth do you mean? I'm not looking behind me. Do you think I have eyes in the back of my head?"

I passed it up and asked pacifically, "Have you finished your list?"

"It's almost complete." She hesitated and added wistfully, "I wish I didn't have to include Rhynda."

Rhynda was John's wife, and I raised my eyebrows. "But of course you can't leave her out."

She made no reply and bent over the pad again, and I stared at the empty fireplace and tried to forget about the logs in the cellar. Presently, she stirred and turned around. "There—it's finished. You take it, my dear, and arrange bedrooms for them while I make out the grocery list."

I took the slip of paper and glanced over it briefly. It was just as I had expected—no extras. John and Rhynda, Berg and Freda Ballinger, John's brother and sister, and Mrs. Ballinger's own personal niece, Amy Perrin. Arranging the rooms was no problem. There were plenty of them; and I simply said eeny, meeny, miney, mo, and got everybody bedded down somewhere. I was pleased to note that Amy had drawn a room that was well away from the bathroom. She was apt to monopolize the bathroom, and there was only one. Mrs. Ballinger would not go to the expense of installing any more, although she could have done it cheaply, had she wanted, by making three modern bathrooms out of the old one.

I stood up and cleared my throat. "May I make a suggestion?"

She swung around and peered at me. "Why, certainly."

"Don't you think you might invite a couple of men friends for your nieces? And perhaps a girl for Berg? It would be more fun for them."

I knew she would refuse, of course. It was as hopeless as asking for the logs would have been, and I merely wondered idly what form her refusal would take.

She tapped her pencil on the desk for a moment, and then shook her head.

"No, I think not. After all, it's just a family party, and in any case, Freda has no men friends."

"I expect Amy would have enough for two," I said mildly.

"I won't have any of Amy's friends coming up here," she retorted sharply.

I gave it up. Even if she had doted on Amy's friends it would mean extra mouths to feed and extra gifts on Christmas. I wondered if she was planning a gift for me and decided that, in any case, I had better get her something that would be appropriate from slave to mistress.

"Have you arranged their bedrooms?" she asked abruptly.

I gave her my plan, and she considered it, foot tapping, and brows drawn together. "Well," she said at last, "I think I'll change that just a little."

She changed it completely, and I was grimly satisfied that Amy's room was still a considerable distance from the bathroom. When that was settled to her satisfaction, she showed me the menu for the Christmas dinner and a neat list of the food she'd have to buy.

I was appalled. The list was about the same as those she had made out for the summer weekends when she had never had more than two of them down at a time.

I pulled myself together and determined to make a stand of some sort. I thought it over for a moment and then said firmly, "Mrs. Ballinger, this is really a very extravagant list."

Her cheeks mottled over with angry red. She knew it was as stingy as she had dared to make it.

"Explain yourself," she said shortly.

I took a long breath, and had time to hope feverishly that I sounded plausible.

"It's simply that you have no fancy extras—I mean, candy, almonds and raisins, things like that. Now I don't believe in foolish waste, myself, but people expect that sort of thing at Christmas. I'm afraid your relatives will think that you've simply forgotten about those things, and probably they'll go to the grocery and charge all sorts of expensive things to your account, and they'll suppose that they're helping you. If you order them yourself, you can keep the expense down to a minimum."

"Rubbish!" she said promptly. "They would not dare to use my account."

I waited while she turned her pencil nervously in her fingers. Presently, with every sign of weakening, she observed, "They know I would not tolerate such a thing." I continued to wait, and at last she held out her hand and said gloomily, "Give me back the list."

I returned it silently and peering over her shoulder watched her add, "One bag peanuts, one bottle hard candy (small), one packet raisins."

"What about a bottle of inexpensive wine?" I murmured hopefully.

But she had been pushed to the limit. "No," she said with finality. "They are not coming down here to drink."

I thought violently, "What the hell are they coming down for?" and felt somewhat relieved.

She put the pencil and pad away carefully and stood up. "Time for bed," she announced crisply.

I longed to say, "Time to stop burning the living-room lights, you mean," but controlled myself and followed her dutifully out into the hall.

Halfway up the stairs, she said suddenly, "You know, I've a good mind to put the whole thing off."

"You can't!" I said desperately. "I mean, how can you? You told them about it last summer, all of them, and they said it would be lovely, and they're—they must be counting on it. Made their plans, you know."

She continued to mount in grim silence, and I cast about in my mind wildly for something more convincing. I felt that spending Christmas alone with Mabel Ballinger was simply too much to put up with.

"The roof," I said suddenly. "It's leaking badly. And John promised to fix it at Christmas. You can hardly ask him without the others."

"Yes—well, yes, I suppose you're right. I'll have to go through with it."

I sighed with relief and was shortly to regret bitterly that I had ever thought of the roof. She reached the top step with a grunt, and I pressed close behind her. We both stood for a moment, looking down the great shadowy, empty hall, listening to the wind which was now howling around outside the house. Then we started slowly towards our bedrooms, which adjoined.

We had gone about halfway when we heard the noise.

It seemed to be directly over our heads, and it was a sort of dragging sound, as though something heavy and soft were being pulled jerkily along the attic floor.

We waited, petrified, until it had stopped, and then I looked at her fearfully. I decided in a panic that if she told me to go up to the attic and investigate I would refuse point-blank.

She turned her head away from me and shivered and pulled her knitted wool scarf more closely around her. "Rats," she said faintly. "I—we must put traps up there, in the morning."

She laid an unsteady hand on my arm and drew me into her bedroom.

I switched on her bedroom lamp and turned down the bed while she watched me with eyes that didn't really see me. She shivered again, and I said as cheerfully as I could, "How about a hot-water bottle for your feet? It's cold up here."

She shook her head vaguely. "I think it must have been rats, don't you? I mean, old houses always have rats, don't they? And rats can make an astounding noise. Or squirrels. Do you think it might be squirrels?"

I did not think it had been either rats or squirrels—it had sounded much too heavy—but I wanted to be reassuring, for I was afraid she was going to ask me to spend the night in her room. I was shaking slightly with nervousness, myself, but I much preferred my own bed and room.

So I said heartily, "Oh yes, either rats or squirrels. Those things can make an awful racket, and it always sounds louder when the house is quiet."

I decided to get Doris, the cook, who slept on the ground floor, to come up to the attic with me first thing in the morning for an investigation.

Mrs. Ballinger had seated herself on the end of the bed, her fingers gripping the post. There was an interval of uneasy silence, and then I said firmly, "Well, good night, Mrs. Ballinger. I hope you sleep well."

She did not seem to hear, and I started for the door. As my hand fell on the knob, she roused and called sharply, "Wait! Come back."

I turned back reluctantly and stood a few feet from her in an attitude of respectful impatience. She was looking straight ahead of her. "It wasn't rats, and you know it as well as I do. It was the old man."

I felt the prickle of hair along my scalp, and I had to swallow twice before I asked hollowly, "What old man?"

She faced me then and looked at me queerly for a moment. I braced myself and remembered that she was always running to cheap fortune-tellers and sending for her horoscope. She was intensely superstitious.

"Have you never heard the story connected with this house?" she asked slowly.

I said I hadn't—and refrained from adding that I didn't want to hear it. She gripped the mahogany poster of the bed more firmly. "It happened close on a hundred years ago. Edward Ballinger lived here then—he was over ninety—and he lived alone, except for several servants.

"He went up to the attic one day—no one knows why—and while he was up there, he fell off a chair and broke his leg. He apparently called for help but could not make himself heard, and he was there for several hours before he was discovered. A housemaid eventually heard him trying to drag himself across the floor towards the stairs.

"She called the other servants, and they carried him down and put him to bed, but when the doctor arrived, he pronounced him dead. I don't know what room he died in. I wish I did. It might even be this one."

She glanced around her fearfully, and I said quickly, "Oh well, it doesn't really matter. You've probably slept in a good many rooms where people have died."

"Yes, but an ordinary death. This is different. The servants covered him with a sheet and left him, but when they showed the undertaker in early the following morning, they found, to their horror, that the old man was lying on the floor over on the other side of the room. They sent for the doctor, but the doctor said, again, that he was dead,and swore that he had been dead the first time."

She fell silent, and I moved uncomfortably. "The doctor was probably saving his own face," I said flatly.

She shrugged. "In any case, the story goes that if ever there is a dragging noise across the attic floor it means that a Ballinger will meet with a fatal accident, and if you don't watch the body until it is buried, it will walk."

"Walk?"

"Walk," she repeated firmly.

"Where?" I asked, feeling silly.

She became more normal then. "How do I know?" she said impatiently. "It just walks, that's all. You'd better go to bed now. I'm going to lock my door, and I advise you to do the same. Good night."

I went out, wondering vaguely what good a locked door was supposed to be against a hundred-year-old ghost. The absurdity of it made me feel better.

I stood in the hall for a while, looking uncertainly down its dim length. I wanted to slide quickly into my room and lock the door, but I was in the habit of going down to the kitchen each night after Mrs. Ballinger went to bed and making myself a little supper, and I felt that it would be pure sissy to give in.

I squared my shoulders and went to the kitchen. I turned on all the lights and made quite a clatter and tried not to think about how ghastly it would be if an old man came sidling through the swinging door from the pantry.

I ate my supper quickly and told myself that it was because I was hungry. I was clearing away the few dishes, when an unmistakable sound from the front of the house caused me to stand stockstill.

I distinctly heard cautious footsteps descend the stairs and cross the hall—and then the front door was opened and closed again with a faint click.

CHAPTER
2

MY COURAGE DESERTED me, and leaving the dishes where they were, I flew upstairs and locked myself in my room. I sat on my bed and pictured an old, old man, with a broken leg, walking down the stairs and out the front door. It was so silly that I laughed at it, and then found I was laughing a bit too heartily, so I pulled myself up and went to bed.

The sun shining in my window the following morning half convinced me that I had only imagined that quiet exit from the house. I told Mrs. Ballinger about it, but she merely said, "Nonsense. You were nervous after hearing that noise in the attic." While the sun continued to shine, I believed her, but nightfall made me uneasy again.

There was a great deal of work to do that week. The house had to be cleaned up a bit. I didn't bother with dark corners or getting behind the ancient upright piano, but Doris and I tried to polish the parts that showed.

Doris was sent out to chop down a fir tree, and I was delegated to buy some cheap gifts, which I tried to choose carefully so that they would look more expensive. Mrs. Ballinger wanted to string popcorn as sole trimming for the tree, but I told her that popcorn was very high right now and that people were economizing by buying their trimmings at the five-and-ten.

I shopped carefully and bought wrapping paper and decorations, and Doris and I worked hard for several days fixing things up. By Wednesday, December 23, the place looked almost festive. Mrs. Ballinger was pleased because it looked as though a lot more money had been spent than she had actually parted with. I was pleased too and felt that I had latent talent as a magician.

We were in good spirits that night at dinner and were actually chatting amiably when the first telegram arrived. Mrs. Ballinger took it over the telephone, and I could tell by her voice that something

had upset her badly. She came back to the table with an air of tragedy, and I felt sure that one of the nieces or nephews had been
injured.

"Bad news?" I asked, bracing myself for the worst.

"Yes." She sat down heavily and stared dully at her coffee.

"Who—?"

"Berg."

"Oh. I'm sorry." I really meant it. Berg was always so gay, laughing and carrying on.

"What—what happened?" I asked timidly.

"He's bringing a friend with him."

"He's—what?" I gasped, staring at her.

"He's bringing a friend. He has absolutely no right to do it. I
never said he could, and I resent it." She rattled her spoon violently
in her coffee cup. "Jones," she muttered. "Such a common name."

"Jones?" I repeated feebly. I was still trying to readjust my men-
tal picture of Berg lying near death on a hospital cot.

"Berg's friend. His name is Richard Jones. I'd have changed it if
it were mine."

I elevated my nose and made no reply. My name is Leigh Smith.

She glanced up at me. "You might as well take that expression off
your face, my dear. I know your name is Smith, and I would have
changed that too."

"How about Schmaltz?" I said bitterly.

"Save your sarcasm." She finished her coffee and set the cup
down with a bang. "Well, we've plenty of bedrooms, and we'll simply
have to serve the food out in smaller portions, for I won't buy more."

She cheered up a bit after that, and we shifted to the living room
But she was in for a bad time. Two telegrams followed in swift succes-
sion.

The first was from Rhynda, stating briefly that she was bringing a
Mrs. Rosalie Hannahs. The second informed us that Amy would be
accompanied by a Mr. Donald Tait.

Mrs. Ballinger was almost hysterical. "I'll have to phone them,"
she said wildly. "I can't possibly have all those extra people."

"The phone bills," I said hastily. "They'd come to more than the
extra food."

She admitted it quite simply and sat down heavily on a chair,
with despair on her face. She was silent for some time, and I re-

flected pleasantly that it would be nice to see some new faces, but I kept my expression grave and a little sad.

Mrs. Ballinger spoke suddenly. "I'll send them all telegrams—or night letters. Aren't night letters cheaper? That'll get them in time."

"You can't," I said desperately. "They'll merely pretend that they never received them. Or they'll get mad and won't come themselves, and all this food and stuff will be wasted. And the roof will still leak."

She glared at me angrily and then resumed her look of despair.

"Look here," I said, after a moment, "I have it all figured out. You give me four dollars and thirty-nine cents, and I'll get the extra food and three gifts, and that will be the entire outlay."

She said three times that it could not be done, and then she handed out the money and cheered up.

I took the bus into the village the following morning and spent fifteen dollars. I used my own money to make up the difference— kissed it good-by and hoped the party would be worth it.

I hurried home, wrapped up the three gifts, and then flew around getting the extra bedrooms ready. After a bite of lunch, I dressed myself nicely, and thoroughly enjoyed having something to dress for again. I got downstairs just in time to greet the first arrivals. They were John and Rhynda Ballinger, Freda Ballinger, and Rhynda's friend Mrs. Rosalie Hannahs.

Freda kissed her aunt, shook hands with me, and then stepped to one side. People rarely noticed her much. She was not good-looking, she did not dress well, and her personality was rather colorless. I did observe, though, that she had done herself up a bit this time. She wore a bright green coat, orange wool scarf and gloves, and a multicolored woolen cap in which the predominant color, unfortunately, was blue.

Rhynda, of course, looked smart and attractive as always. She was dressed in darkish, expensive-looking tweeds, and her auburn hair, under a striking felt hat, gave a more effective color note than all Freda's ensemble.

Mrs. Hannahs appeared to be somewhere in her forties, and her clothes were fussy and far too young for her. She dripped honey on Mrs. Ballinger and said it was sweet of her to put up with a perfect stranger in her lovely old house.

Mrs. Ballinger's smile looked as though she had dropped her face and cracked it. She said, "Not at all," stiffly, and turned immediately to John, who was her favorite.

He was a nice fellow, pleasant and quiet. He would not go out enough to suit Rhynda, and so she had to go with other men, but John never seemed to mind.

In the past six months he had repaired practically the entire house for his aunt and was more firmly her favorite than ever. I think his fondness for tools and the repair jobs he did were his form of recreation. He seemed to find it more restful after business than the social life that interested Rhynda. He often wandered off and set to work as soon as he had taken off his hat and coat. He was good-looking enough, tall and dark, but faintly like Freda—a bit colorless.

Mrs. Ballinger kissed him and patted his shoulder. "Where's Berg?" she asked.

"Said he was catching the next train," he told her. "Fellow he's bringing down held him up or something." Mrs. Ballinger frowned briefly at this reference to the unwanted guest and glanced involuntarily at Mrs. Hannahs as being another of the same ilk.

Rhynda pulled off her hat and shook her bright, silky hair back from her face. "Don't worry about Berg. He'll show up sometime, even if it is four o'clock in the morning. Can't we go to our rooms? Maybe Leigh will show us where we belong."

"Of course," I said, and led the way upstairs.

I didn't particularly care for Rhynda, but at least she was amusing. As we marched along the upstairs hall Mrs. Hannahs said enthusiastically, "What a charming old place!"

"It's freezing up here," Rhynda declared, and pulled her coat around her. I visualized the flimsy, delicate underthings she was probably wearing and was glad I had come to realize, early on, that residence in Mrs. Ballinger's house and woolen underwear went strictly hand in hand. I put them into their rooms and hurried down again, for I had heard a car in the drive.

Amy and her Mr. Donald Tait were in the hall. They had driven up in Mr. Tait's car, and both the car and Mr. Tait were long, handsome, and well fitted out. I took them upstairs, and there was trouble immediately.

"I won't be all this distance from the bathroom, such as it is," Amy declared. "What else have you got?" She walked down the hall and went into the room connecting with Mr. Tait's that I had prepared for Mr. Jones. "What's wrong with this?"

"It's a man's room," I explained. "It was furnished for a man. The other has been furnished for a lady. Chintz curtains, you know, and a—a doll sitting on the bed. Mrs. Ballinger dressed it herself. I can't usher Mr. Jones into a room with a doll sitting on the bed."

"Then take the doll out," she said shortly. "I'm staying here."

Donald Tait walked through the connecting door at that point and dropped some of her baggage onto the floor. He disappeared again and returned shortly with another piece, which he threw onto the bed. He went back into his own room and banged the door smartly behind him.

"Seems a trifle put out," I suggested brightly.

"You mind your own business, and get out of here," she said viciously.

I went to the door and opened it. "Shall I bring you the doll? I don't believe Mr. Jones is going to care for it."

She opened her mouth, but I slid out quickly. I went along the hall feeling like a well-trained servant, and as such, meditating on the various merits of spitting in her soup, putting crumbs in her bed, and making the bed with the sheet hanging down on one side and the blanket on the other. I turned to descend the stairs, with my mouth watering, and bumped into a strange man.

I knew it must be the Jones man because Berg was right behind him.

Berg said, "Well, Smithy! How are you, darling?" and planted an audible kiss on my forehead.

He was different from his brother and sister, better looking and with much more personality. They were both dark and inclined to be heavy. His figure was slim and hard, and he had reddish hair.

Mr. Jones had dark hair, which was inclined to be curly, and very blue eyes. When Berg introduced us he bent low over my hand and murmured, "Charmed."

I patted his head and said, "What pretty curls. Are they natural?"

He straightened up and raised one eyebrow.

Berg shook his head. "You shouldn't have mentioned it, Smithy. He's needing a new permanent, and he's sensitive about it."

Berg always used the same room and even kept some of his things in it, and it suddenly occurred to me that it would be better to put the stranger into Berg's unquestionably masculine bedroom. Berg would understand about Amy. I touched his arm, and when he turned to me, whispered the situation into his ear. He merely laughed at me.

"My dear Smithy, I've done enough for Dick by smuggling him out here over Aunt Mabel's dead body. Let him take whatever room he can get, but it won't be mine."

"He's a low, common sort of fellow," Mr. Jones said easily. "Don't let him embarrass you, Miss Smith. Anything will do for me. If you haven't a bedroom, just give me a blanket and a coat hanger."

"It isn't that bad," I said, in some confusion. "I have a room for you, if you care to use it."

I threw open the door and ushered them in. They stood looking at it for a while in silence, and then they turned and looked at each other.

"The doll," said Mr. Jones gravely, "was very thoughtful. I can't sleep properly unless I take my dolly to bed with me."

"None of your foul saloon talk here," Berg said severely. "Not in front of the lady."

"You can put the doll and the fancy cushions in the cupboard," I said hastily. "You're supposed to dress for dinner and be downstairs for tomato juice cocktails at a quarter to seven."

Mr. Jones turned a very blue stare on me and murmured, "A jest, Miss Smith?"

"Grim reality," said Berg gloomily. "There'll be no liquor while you're under this roof, unless it's bootleg."

"In that case," said Mr. Jones pleasantly, "I shall see you—and the tomato juice—at a quarter to seven."

I went off downstairs and collected Mrs. Ballinger, who was wandering around aimlessly, and brought her up to dress for dinner. I put her into her room and then raced for the bathroom, and just made it.

I hurried through the necessary ablutions, but when I opened the door I was shocked to find four people standing in line. Richard Jones was first, Berg stood behind him, Rhynda was behind Berg, sitting on a chair from Mr. Jones's room, and Donald Tait stood behind Rhynda. He appeared vastly more cheerful.

They surveyed me solemnly, and I said with dignity, "I'm sorry that most of you have to stand. I'll have a row of chairs put here tomorrow."

We all laughed then, and they tossed up to see whether Rhynda or the three men should get the bathroom next. Rhynda won, and the men marched down the back stairs in search of what they called the kitchen pump.

I hurried on down the hall, but as I was passing Amy's room I heard raised voices. I slowed down and distinctly heard Freda say, "Amy, you are one of the vilest creatures on God's earth. He will surely punish you, and so will I. So be prepared."

I thought I heard her coming towards the door then, so I went on quickly.

CHAPTER
3

I DRESSED QUICKLY AND with a feeling of pleasant excitement. It seemed to me that it might be quite a nice party.

I knew there would be a lot of work. Aall the bedrooms were occupied except the little room at the end of the hall, and it wasn't really a bedroom. We called it the sewing room, although nobody ever bothered to sew in it. Mrs. Ballinger had opened up the parlor, which was a young ballroom, and the dining room, which looked like an old-fashioned banqueting hall.

I brushed away the thought of all the housework that would have to be done and made up my mind to have a good time this one night, at any rate. I put on my best evening dress, a really good one that I had bought just before my father died, and I spent a lot of time on my hair and face.

As I descended the stairs, I couldn't help wishing that there was someone standing at the bottom to appreciate the picture I made. There was no one around, though, so I made for the kitchen to see how Doris was getting on with the dinner. She assured me that she had everything under control, but I lingered for a while because the stove made the room comfortably warm and I was chilled through.

Doris plodded about contentedly between stove and table. Nothing ever seemed to bother her much. She slept in a room off the kitchen and apparently spent most of her time between the two. She never went out unless it was absolutely necessary, and on her days off she usually had friends or relatives come to visit.

As I watched her, it suddenly occurred to me that it might have been one of her friends who had been in the attic that night and who had subsequently departed quietly by way of the front door. The idea relieved me vastly, for the thing had been nagging at my mind all the week.

I realized with satisfaction that the housework was all that need worry me. I had just turned to leave when I heard the sound of coal being shoveled in the cellar, and I spun around to stare at Doris in consternation.

She spread her hands out and shrugged. "I told them. I said nobody was supposed to touch the furnace, only you or me, but Mr. Berg said it wasn't any work for ladies, and that Mr. Jones backed him up. I told them there was only enough coal to the end of the week, but they just laughed and said they'd put back all they used."

I couldn't help laughing, although I knew we'd have to spend a week shivering in a cold house after they had left. However, the immediate prospect of adequate warmth was cheering, and I went on through the swinging door to the butler's pantry, humming to myself.

Unexpectedly, I came upon Mr. Jones mixing cocktails. I stopped short and stared at him.

"Where did you get it?" I whispered.

"Bought it," he said cheerfully.

I thought of the grocery store that had Mrs. Ballinger's account and asked feebly, "Where?"

He glanced at me and smiled faintly. "At a liquor emporium in some small town on the way out."

"You came by car?"

He set the bottle down and turned full upon me. "Not only that, but my mother's maiden name was Phoebe Wright; my father's name was David Jones; I was born in New York City on the ninth day of June 1908; I am not an anarchist nor am I a polygamist; and I have no present plans to overthrow the government."

I felt my face grow hot and I said resentfully, "If you'd been in moth balls as long as I have—"

He patted my head paternally. "Peace, Smithy."

I laughed and said, "All right. Here, let me help you with that."

We took the two glass pitchers that had to serve as cocktail shakers into the parlor, and I brought out some long-unused wineglasses. Freda had come down, dressed in a cheap, ill-fitting evening gown of bright red. John was there, too, either looking into space or at a crack in the wall which needed repairing.

I looked at the huge Christmas tree, the gaily wrapped parcels beneath it, and could hardly believe that we had spent so little money on it all. I had arranged the table in the dining room during the morning, and I glanced in to admire it afresh. It looked so impressive that I lingered at the door, wondering what sort of startling show I could have put on if I had any real money to spend on it.

Richard Jones materialized at my side with a cocktail and a pair of faintly elevated brows.

"It is for the guests to admire the decorations," he suggested, offering the cocktail and keeping the brows in the air.

I took the drink and made a face at him. "Then why don't you?"

"I've been admiring you," he said impersonally, "so I haven't got around to them yet. I like blond hair with brown eyes, and your skin is ivory rather than pink and white, which is as it should be. You have a very pretty little figure too, and your hair has glints in it, which is vastly better than the dull type of blond hair."

"How embarrassing, if I'd been born a brunette," I murmured.

I caught sight of Berg staggering towards the fireplace with a load of logs, and I hurried after him.

"My God, Berg," I said in an undertone, "those logs are like gold bricks around here. There'll be a row."

He dropped the logs onto the hearth with a crash, and squatting down, began busily to put a fire together.

"If the dear old soul squawks," he said out of the side of his mouth, "tell her the wood caught fire in the cellar, and I brought the logs up to the fireplace so that they would not be wasted. I've made up my mind that this party is going to be a success in spite of her."

I left him with a shrug. I couldn't blame him. I felt the same way about the party.

Freda was sitting against the wall, looking a perfect example of the "I don't smoke, drink, or pet" class, in spite of the red dress. I felt a spasm of pity for her, and I went over and whispered to her to come and find a comfortable chair in front of the fire before they were all taken. She followed me docilely and seated herself rather stiffly in an armchair in front of the blaze that Berg had produced from the dry old logs.

Rhynda came down, and I could see that she was annoyed at not being the last. I felt sure she had waited until she thought her arch-enemy, Amy, had gone down. But apparently Amy had outwaited her.

We started to have a good time. Richard Jones and Berg had had a few cocktails. I was on my second. Rhynda, looking very lovely in an exotic evening gown, in which she was probably freezing to death, tossed off three drinks in about as many minutes. Freda sat upright in the armchair and seemed to be studying her shoes.

We were laughing and talking when Amy came in with Donald Tait, and they were hardly noticed, which was exactly what Rhynda wanted, I suppose. Amy looked interesting and bizarre, as usual. She was not half as good-looking as Rhynda, but her bad points—the too-large nose and the too-thin lips—were so expertly minimized that you scarcely noticed them. Her figure was actually a bit too meager, but she was draped in an expensive silver lame gown that rounded her out very cleverly. She had heavy black hair and very large, dark eyes. Her eyes were her best feature.

I had forgotten Mrs. Ballinger entirely, and it was not until some ten minutes later, at the height of the noise and gaiety, that I suddenly caught sight of her standing at the door in her black lace gown and looking thunder at all of us. I remembered that I was supposed to have hooked her into her dress, and I realized resignedly that I was in for it.

She beckoned to me imperiously, and I went to her, absent-mindedly carrying my glass with me. A mistake, of course. She looked me over from head to foot.

"I'm surprised at you, and disappointed in you, Leigh. I never thought you'd drink that stuff. And why didn't you come to hook me up? I had a dreadful time. And who lit that fire? You know very well we don't need a fire in here."

"I didn't light the fire, Mrs. Ballinger," I said hastily. "I'm sorry about it, but Berg seemed to want it—"

"Where did they get the ingredients for those cocktails?" she interrupted fiercely. "They must have brought the liquor with them. Certainly I have none in the house. But I know you can't make cocktails with liquor alone, you have to use other things. Now, what was it they used?"

I stood before her in helpless silence, thinking of the mounds of empty orange halves that had been piled up around the Jones man in the butler's pantry. I knew we'd have to go without fruit for break-fast.

My mind flew around like a squirrel in a cage and came to no conclusion. And then someone touched my arm, and I turned to see Richard Jones bowing ceremoniously.

"Mrs. Ballinger, I want to offer my profound thanks for this charm-ing party. Such a charming old house, and such a—er—charming hostess. It makes me a little dizzy."

"That's not the charm, that's the cocktails," I said out of the side of my mouth. He was putting it on so thickly that I felt a bit embar-rassed for him. But a glance at Mrs. Ballinger showed me that she had swallowed it whole. She was positively glowing, so I slipped away, thankful to have the accounting delayed for a while.

Five minutes later, Doris spoiled the general effect of opulence by shuffling to the door and admitting that she'd finished preparing the dinner. She eyed us for a moment and added a warning that we'd better put down them glasses and come at once or it would be cold.

Doris was a born cook, and the dinner was a success. She had a knack for making tasty dishes from the cheapest of ingredients. By the time we had finished dinner the party was quite hilarious, and when we returned to the parlor Donald Tait produced some brandy.

The Ballingers belonged to that school of thought that holds with opening the packages on Christmas Eve, so we attacked them, and the brandy, together. There is nothing like being a little tight when you open your Christmas presents. Instead of being disappointed with most of the things, you find them all screamingly funny.

All in all, it was a highly successful evening, but there was one incident that lay in my mind and faintly troubled me. I saw Rhynda and Richard Jones with their heads together, clicking their glasses and drinking a toast. His arm was across her shoulders. John was standing directly behind them, staring at them. He was clearly very angry. His hands were clenched, and his face had an ugly expres-sion.

I saw it for only a few seconds, and then Amy and Donald Tait danced past and blocked it from view. When I next had a chance to look, John had left the group and was sitting in a chair, smoking. He looked so much his usual self that I wondered a little if I had been mistaken about it all. But I could not forget it.

I watched Rhynda and Richard after that, and there was no doubt that they were sticking together a great deal. Berg joined them sometimes, but Berg was more or less in circulation, moving around the room from group to group and laughing and joking as he always did.

Amy kept Donald Tait close by her side, which was the usual procedure with Amy and her young men, and possibly the reason for her having a new one every six months or so.

John sat and smoked by himself for a while, and then the next time I noticed him he had drifted into the company of Mrs. Hannahs and was amiably explaining to her exactly what was necessary to be done to eliminate the cracks in the wall.

The combination was short-lived, however. Rhynda noticed it, and edging over to them, deliberately broke it up. She brought John over to the other side of the room, seated him in a chair, kissed the top of his head, ruffled his hair, and rejoined Richard and Berg.

Mrs. Hannahs, looking a trifle forlorn, entered into a desultory conversation with Mrs. Ballinger. Freda circulated aimlessly, and I suspected her of being a bit tight. She was not particularly noticed nor ever welcomed with loud shrieks, like Berg, and she hung around my neck quite a bit.

At half past twelve Mrs. Ballinger started to tell everybody about the noise we had heard in the attic. It took some time, and there was a great deal of repetition before everybody heard it, and Mrs. Ballinger went off to bed immediately afterwards, as though the fatigue had been too much for her.

The party broke up at about half past one, and they all started upstairs in a body. I was about to follow when I remembered that the room would have to be tidy for the morning, and I turned back. I had started getting things to rights when Richard put his head around the door.

"Party's over, Smithy," he observed. "Look behind you, and you'll find the crowd has gone."

I continued to sort glasses and empty ashtrays and said, without looking up, "I'm coming in just a minute."

He followed his head into the room, murmured, "Tch, tch. You women!" and began to help me.

Rhynda was back before I could say anything.

"What are you doing, Jonesy?" she called.

"Helping Smith with the housework," he said cheerfully.

She drew in a breath of impatience and said crossly, "Oh, for heaven's sake! She's paid to do it, and you're not!"

I colored painfully and fumbled an ashtray so that the butts spilled over onto the floor. I heard him say coolly, "Go to bed, Rhynda," and she flounced out with an angry exclamation.

The room seemed to emerge clean and tidy in no time, after that. Richard was very expert, and he told me, in explanation, that he had once had a bachelor apartment with no service.

It could not have been more than ten minutes more before we put out the lights and started up the stairs. I was conscious of a high wind blowing furiously outside. In the upper hall we came unexpectedly upon a little knot of people talking together. I don't now remember who they were, because at that moment there came distinctly a sound of something dragging across the attic floor above us.

Some woman gave a little scream, and then they were all out of their rooms, standing in the drafty hall and gaping at the ceiling while the noise dragged its way slowly and intermittently across the attic.

CHAPTER
4

RICHARD JONES BROKE the spell by saying cheerfully, "Let's investigate. Where is the door to the attic, Miss Smith?"

"This way," John said laconically. He led the way to the stairs, and Richard, Berg and Donald Tait followed in a body.

I looked around then to see who was left and found that everyone was there with the exception of Mrs. Ballinger, who was a heavy sleeper. I shivered a little and asked uncertainly, "When did you first hear it ?"

Freda, her hair in a pigtail, her face pallid, and her figure shapeless in a plaid woolen dressing gown, spoke in a high, shaking voice. "You know what it means, don't you? It means that a Ballinger will die by accident."

"Don't be silly," I said quickly. "How can you believe all that rubbish?"

"It's all very well for you," she whined and was interrupted by the return of the three men from the attic.

"Nothing up there but dust and junk," Berg said, as we waited breathlessly. "Guess it was just one of those unexplainable noises that you always hear in very old houses."

Well, it was true that you often heard queer noises in old places,and yet I could not feel quite satisfied about it. But I was dead tired, and I slept like a log until the alarm clock roused me at eight o'clock. I dressed quickly and carefully and crept out of my room with a smock and dust cap under my arm. I knew there was an appalling amount of housework to be done, but I did not want to be too obvious about it. The smock and dust cap were easily removable at any given moment, and the second layer was a smart jersey sports dress.

John was my only companion at breakfast. He said he was anxious to get at the leak in the roof. I thought of Freda, shivering and muttering about an accident to one of the Ballingers, and though I am not at all superstitious, I was conscious of a faint, unreasonable shadow of fear. I found myself trying to dissuade him.

"Why don't you leave it until some other time, John? It's—it's Christmas, you know, and it's cold. You could do it in the spring, when it's warmer."

He drained his coffee cup, lit a cigarette, and said easily, "Oh, it won't take long. I'd just as soon do that as anything else."

I sighed and suppressed an inclination to suggest that he make a temporary job from the inside. I knew he was looking forward to the work and would probably be quite happily occupied for the rest of the day. We had had no snow, and although it was cold, the roof was quite dry, and he was always careful. He would put in new shingles so methodically and so perfectly that it would be pure pleasure for him to look at them after they were done. John was like that.

We were preparing to leave the dining room when Mrs. Ballinger sailed in. I glanced at her guiltily and was thankful that she had not heard me trying to toss away a free repair job.

She was in a good mood and invited us to keep her company while she ate her breakfast. But when she heard that John was on his way to the roof, and I to do battle with vast expanses of dust and disorder, she let us go with a blessing. She loved to have people working busily for her.

I tackled the downstairs rooms first and did not even try to be thorough. I went through them like a breeze and worked my way up the stairs, along the upper hall, and to the bathroom, where I met a snag. The door was locked, and I could hear the sound of running water. I felt sure that it was Amy.

I was tired by that time, so I went to my room, stretched out on the bed, and lit a cigarette. A glance at my wristwatch showed me that it was half past twelve, and I groaned as I realized that none of the bedrooms were done yet.

I heard the faint, muffled thud of John's hammer, and the sound made me restless and uneasy. I looked at my watch again, and decided, with a little breath of relief, that if he were to have time to wash up before lunch, I'd have to call him now. I crushed out my cigarette and started for the attic.

I was sorry before I was halfway up the stairs that I had not gone outside to call him. The place was dim and vast and stretched away into shadowy corners. I advanced gingerly, thinking consciously of spiders and rats because I did not want to be silly enough to think of the hunched figure of an old man dragging a useless leg.

I went to the spot that seemed to be directly under John's hammer. The noise was much louder here, a regular banging that seemed to shake the whole roof. I waited for an interval and then called him and told him the time. He answered me and promised to come at once.

I got down the attic stairs again in about half the time it I had taken me to go up, and I flew along to the men's bedrooms, made their beds, and tidied up sketchily. I returned to the hall and was astounded to find the bathroom unoccupied. I made a dash for it and locked the door firmly behind me.

I washed up the bathroom and myself, in the order named, and had just finished when I heard Doris pounding the luncheon gong. As I came out, I bumped into Rhynda. I murmured an apology and started to pass her, but she caught my arm.

"Leigh, wait a minute. I'm sorry about what I said last night. I was a pig. We all should have helped you. Mabel has no right to expect you to do all that. It's ridiculous! It was a darned nice party you fixed for us, and I want you to know that I appreciate it."

I murmured something deprecatory, and she stepped hastily inside the bathroom door as some sort of movement was heard from Amy's room. She made a little face in that direction and added, "I don't know about Amy—you know how she is—but Freda and I have made up our rooms, so you won't have to bother about them."

"It's awfully nice of you," I said, and meant it.

Rhynda could be very sweet and considerate, if she were in the mood, but she was apt to be extremely nasty if she were sufficiently annoyed. I suppose that she must have been annoyed when she made that remark the previous night. But why? It did not interest me much, in any case, so I forgot about it and went down to lunch.

Only Mrs. Bailinger, John and I had any appetite for the meal, as the others had all had late breakfasts. It was just as well, too, because it was the remains of the chickens from the night before and there wasn't very much. I knew the bones were destined for soup at dinner and I wondered whether even Doris's ingenuity could produce much flavor from the two bleached-looking skeletons that were left.

Rosalie Hannahs disposed of the bits and pieces on her plate and then took a long breath and said brightly, "I declare, I wish I could stay in this lovely old house for a month. It certainly would take the wrinkles out of my soul."

She glanced at Mrs. Ballinger, whose return stare said more plainly than words, "Nothing doing."

"I'm staying for a week, anyway," Berg said chattily. "Until after New Year's. Dick will be able to make it, too. Men of leisure, you know."

Mrs. Ballinger gasped and said desperately, "But, Berg, what about your business? Surely they won't allow you the whole week?"

He balanced a spoon across the tip of his finger and said, "Oh yes. In fact, they insisted upon it."

"But you had your vacation last summer," his aunt said sharply.

"They think I need a longer one. In fact, they made rather a point of suggesting that I don't show up again until they hold open house for the alumni."

Rhynda said, "Oh, Berg!" in a tone of impatience, and John frowned and shook his head. Mrs. Ballinger got it after a moment of concentration.

"You've been discharged!"

"And they needn't think I don't know why, either," Berg said darkly, dropping the teaspoon and fishing for a cigarette. "I know all about it, and someday I'll face them with it."

"What do you mean?" John asked, beginning to be interested.

"I mean, I know why I got the bird. I know all about it."

"Let's hear," said John, preparing for a tale of intricate office intrigue.

"They caught me doing the Suzy Q. during office hours."

John said, "Oh, shut up," Rhynda giggled, and Mrs. Ballinger who had been tch-tching for some time looked puzzled. Any loss of money coming in seemed a tragic thing to her. She could not imagine jesting about it.

The three Ballingers, Freda, John and Berg, had a private income of about seventy-five dollars a month each left in a trust fund for them by their father so that they would never be actually destitute. Freda had an office job of some sort and managed her finances quite competently. John was doing well in a bank, but Berg drifted around from one thing to another. I think he had been almost everything from an actor to a cowboy. He had a lively interest in anything that was new, and I believe he liked nothing better than to be fired from a job that had begun to pall.

Mrs. Ballinger stopped clicking her tongue long enough to inquire thinly how it was that Mr. Jones was able to absent himself from the daily grind for an entire week. She did not ask him if he had been fired, too, but it hung in the air.

He smiled sunnily and said that he thought his concern could do very well—nay, better—without him.

Mrs. Hannahs chirruped, "I'm sure you're being too modest, Mr. Jones."

Mr. Jones winked at her, to her confusion, and John stirred and observed, "I'll have to go back, worse luck. But there's no reason why Rhynda and Rosalie can't stay."

I dared not look at Mrs. Ballinger. I knew that she must be dangerously close to the explosion point, and I wondered nervously whether John was deliberately exasperating her, or whether he could possibly be so completely blind. To take his free repair work, and himself—who was her favorite—off and leave all these drones on her hands was nothing short of high treason. I think she would certainly have made a scene had it not been for Doris, who opportunely took that moment to spill hot coffee all down the front of Amy's dress.

Amy sprang up, shouting abuse, and Doris, mopping at her ineffectually with a napkin, declared earnestly that in all her years of service she had never done such a crude thing before. Being practically in the servant class myself I knew perfectly well that Doris had done it on purpose, and I could not find it in my heart to blame her. It was the only way to square things with Amy, who was not only inconsiderate at all times but downright objectionable to those who she thought were her inferiors.

When the fuss had died down and they had all left the dining room, I asked Doris if I could help with the dishes, but she shook her head firmly. "No, dearie—you run along and leave all this to me. You're doin' plenty, Lord knows, and you're only young once."

I thanked her, and she went out into the kitchen, and then I heard the muffed hammer strokes from the roof again. I put my hands over my ears for a moment, hating to think of John perched up there, and telling myself at the same time not to be silly, because the roof was not slippery and John was always careful.

I shook myself and went up to Amy's room, because I knew that her bed would be still unmade. I made it, with the sheet hanging down one side and the blankets down the other, and met Amy coming in as I was on my way out.

"What are you doing in here?" she asked sharply.

"I was making your bed," I said, matching her tone, "but if you prefer to do it yourself, I shall be glad to leave it to you."

"Oh no," she said quickly. "No, that's all right. Do it, by all means."

I went on down the hall to Mrs. Hannahs' room and glanced in. As I had expected, it was in apple pie order. That finished the work for the time being, and I went to my own room and fell onto the bed. The sound of hammering came faintly to my ears as I went off to sleep.

I was awakened by a loud bang on the door and called feebly, "Come in."

Berg walked in and perched himself on the end of my bed.

"Listen, darling, Doris is about to serve a sumptuous tea, after which she is quitting us cold for the rest of the day. She says she has her own Christmas to celebrate. She is leaving a kettle of soup on the stove, and we are to help ourselves from it, when and if we get hungry, later on. Further, we are not to bother you about it. My guess is that she likes you, and only you, out of this whole gang."

"Don't chatter so, Berg," I said sleepily. "John's still hammering, isn't he? Is he never going to stop?"

"Not," said Berg solemnly, "until the last shingle is perfectly and prettily in its place. He's got to stick at it, too, because he has to go back to the city next week, and if this job isn't done Mabel'll sue him for breach of promise."

I stretched and swung my feet over the edge of the bed.

"Are you coming, Smithy?" Berg asked plaintively. "Or must I go alone to battle with Amy over the biggest piece of gingerbread? Greedy hog," he added without venom.

"You go and round up the others, Berg. I'll go to the attic and call John. We might as well have the tea while it's hot."

He went off, and I hurried up to the attic, feeling very brave because it was the second time I had forced myself up there. I went to the spot where he was hammering, and when he paused, opened my mouth to call him.

But I never got that far.

I heard the hammer fall against the shingles and heard it clatter down the side of the roof. There was a rending of wood, a hoarse shout from John, and the sickening thud and bump of his body as it went down the steep incline.

CHAPTER
5

THE SILENCE THAT followed those dreadful sounds was so heavy that I was acutely conscious of the chattering of my own teeth. For a moment, I could not seem to move or breathe. Then I gasped and flew to the stairs.

I flung into Rosalie Hannahs' room, threw open the window, and looked out. I could see John lying down there, his body curiously twisted and very still, and I had a vague, horrified impression that there was blood around his head.

I drew back in again and stood for a moment leaning against the sill, my hands over my face, and my heart thudding dully.

"Whatever in the world is the matter?" said an amazed voice, and I looked up to see Mrs. Hannahs standing at the dressing table, powder puff suspended, and her face only half on.

"It's John," I whispered. "Don't let Rhynda see it."

I started for the door and heard her let out a shrill scream behind me. I turned hastily and saw her hanging out the window, her plump body heaving with shriek after shriek. I dragged her in, shut her up somehow, and left her lying on the bed moaning.

I rushed to the stairs and started down and saw that they were all grouped in the lower hall, looking up at me.

"It's John," I said breathlessly. "Out at the side," and gestured feebly.

Richard and Berg were out of the front door without a moment's delay, and Freda was close behind them. Amy and Donald Tait followed more slowly, but Mrs. Ballinger and Rhynda just stood there and looked at me mutely. I avoided their eyes, and brushing past them, hurried to the telephone and called for a doctor.

As I hung up the receiver, Mrs. Ballinger gave a little moan and fainted dead away. Doris appeared from the kitchen before I could open my mouth to call her and took in the situation in one competent glance.

"Pick up her legs," she said practically, and herself grasped the inert form firmly by the shoulders.

We carried her to a couch, and Doris went off for some smelling salts, after stuffing a couple of pillows under her feet so that her head would hang down. I chafed at her wrists as best I could.

Rhynda continued to stand perfectly still, her face deadly white and her eyes very dark and bright. She spoke suddenly.

"Leigh! You go out and see what it is. Find out, and come back and tell me. Somebody *must* tell me. I'll—I'll go crazy."

I thought she looked ripe for violent hysterics at any minute, and I did not want to set her off, so I dropped Mrs. Ballinger's wrists and hurried out the front door. I went around to the side of the house and saw that Richard and Donald Tait were just lifting John from the ground. Berg stood a little apart, his face very white and set, and Freda was sobbing on his shoulder.

He looked up at me and said desperately, "Leigh, take her in, will you?"

I disentangled Freda from him and started off with an arm about her waist. We had not gone far when I stumbled on something and discovered with a little thrill of horror that it was John's scaffolding. It was just a wooden plank with an arrangement of ropes which secured it to the chimney and also acted as a pulley, so that he could raise or lower it.

I turned my head and called back to Berg, "Put that thing down in the cellar."

He nodded briefly, and I heard him begin to fumble with it.

I took Freda in, and Richard and Donald carried John to a couch in the parlor. Mrs. Ballinger was sitting up in an armchair, looking pretty rocky, and Rhynda was on her knees beside John, with her face hidden in his coat. Doris stood beside Mrs. Ballinger's chair with her arms folded.

The doorbell rang, and Doris admitted the doctor. We had had no occasion for a doctor before, and I had simply picked one out of the directory, a Dr. Kenneth O'Beirne.

He turned out to be the Village Institution and coroner, and was a big man, youngish and with a pleasant manner. He pronounced John dead, superintended the removal of his body upstairs, and then collected us in the parlor to get the details of the accident, this last in his capacity as coroner. After a few questions, he said he wanted to see where John had fallen, and most of us picked up whatever coat was nearest and escorted him around to the side of the house. I noticed that it was very cold, and that the wind was rising.

"Whereabouts on the roof was he working?" Dr. O'Beirne asked.

Several people started to reply, but Richard Jones got the floor. "I was watching him this morning," he said. "You can just see the pieces of wood he has nailed to the roof, like steps going up. He stood on those and nailed the shingles on to his right. As he got them done, he'd take a step up—you see he has the pieces of wood nailed right to the top of the roof."

Dr. O'Beirne gazed upward for a while and then shook his head. "It's a great pity," he commented. "People should leave this sort of thing to professional builders. They know better how to guard against accidents. He must have slipped and lost his balance."

After a few technicalities he got into his car and drove away.

I was shivering in Mrs. Ballinger's raincoat, the first wrap that had met my eye, and I was glad to get inside again. As I hung the coat up in the hall closet, I suddenly remembered the scaffolding. I wondered whether John had been standing on it when he fell or whether he had been attempting to fix it to the chimney. I had an uneasy feeling that I ought to tell Dr. O'Beirne about it, in any case.

But I forgot about it completely in the next half-hour, for I was too busy to think at all.

Mrs. Ballinger and Rhynda had both retired to bed, and Doris and I rushed to and fro with hot-water bottles, smelling salts and aspirin, and numerous assurances that we would attend to all the arrangements. When we had gotten them quiet we dashed downstairs to try and patch up the tea that Amy had been demanding every time she saw us.

I was trying to eat and drink something and feeling faintly ashamed because I was able to when Berg came to me and mentioned the scaffolding.

"Don't you think we ought to phone O'Beirne and tell him about it?" he asked.

I said tiredly, "What's the use? We don't want him out here again, and the conclusion would be the same—accidental death. After all, the scaffolding can't prove that anyone went up there and pushed him off."

He moved away with a look of pain, and I felt ashamed of myself for not being more tactful. I sighed and took a moment to wish that I were somewhere where people waited on me hand and foot and I never had to lift a finger from morning till night.

I glanced around the room and saw that Amy, Donald and Richard were eating with as good an appetite as mine. Berg stood by a window, staring into space, and Freda was trying to drink hot tea while her tears dripped into it.

Rosalie Hannahs had the floor. She must have been a very old friend of John's, for she was giving his life history from infancy on and making it extremely flattering. She gave herself time out occasionally, to nibble at the food on her plate.

I left when John was about eighteen because I had a restless feeling that I would be wanted. I found Mrs. Ballinger in the upper hall, in her dressing gown. She was highly agitated, and she cried shrilly, "Where have you been, Leigh? I've called and called and could not get anyone to hear."

She was shivering and half-crying, and I put an arm around her and led her back to her own room. "You must go back to bed," I said soothingly. "I'll look after everything."

"But you haven't—you're not. There's no one with him. My poor John! You've left him all alone, and I won't have it! Do you understand? I won't have it!"

"It's all right. I understand. But you must lie down again."

She wrenched herself away and almost screamed at me, "No! No! No! Listen to me, Leigh. Someone must stay with him *all the time.* He *must not be left alone. "*

I could do nothing with her, so in the end I went downstairs and brought Berg up. She made him promise to sit with John and to arrange with the other men to take shifts. I went downstairs again and on the way remembered that no arrangements had been made about the funeral. I changed my course and headed for the telephone.

When I finally replaced the receiver, it was borne in upon me that the house was definitely colder than the usual Ballinger freezing point. I heard the crackle of a fire from the living room and knew that the others would not notice the falling temperature for a while, but there was no time to be lost.

I groaned and rushed to the kitchen, where Doris raised an eyebrow in mute question.

"Furnace," I said briefly, and went on down to the cellar. She followed me, and in fear and trembling we looked at it together. It was dead out. We cursed freely, and while she began to rake out the dead coals, I went to get paper and kindling.

It was a tremendous furnace, and lighting it was something of a tremendous job. We were about halfway through, grimy, sweating, and grimly silent, when Richard Jones appeared on the stairs.

"Thought you must have gone on your vacation, Smithy," he observed. "They're all looking for you, up above."

'"Oh, damn them!" I said crossly.

He came over and relieved Doris of the coal shovel. "Go on up and wash your faces, both of you. And understand that this furnace is my responsibility as long as I'm here. I don't want to catch either one of you mucking around it again."

We thanked him almost tearfully and made a beeline for the stairs. I noticed, as I went up, that John's scaffolding had been put under the stairs. I saw the broken rope that had cost him his life and shivered uncomfortably.

It turned out to be Amy who had made the most determined search for me. She told me, aggrievedly, that there was no hot water. I explained that the hot-water boiler was connected with the furnace, that the furnace had been out for some time, and that she probably would have hot water in two hours' time, unless she cared to go to the kitchen and heat some on the stove.

She gave me an evil look and suggested that I bring pitchers of hot water to the guests' rooms, since I had let the furnace go out. I said I'd be only too glad but that it was not my work, and the servants' union would get at me if I attempted it.

I went to the living room, where Freda sat alone by the fire, knitting. I stood there for a moment, wondering what I should be doing, but when nothing very pressing presented itself, I sat on the edge of a chair and extended my cold hands to the blaze. Freda glanced at me, blew her nose, and began to tell me in a hushed voice a long story about some friends of hers, millionaires or close to it. I caught only snatches of the tale, something about a house they owned that had a roof from which it would be impossible to fall off.

I was nearly asleep, despite the fact that Freda was rapidly approaching the denouement of her story, when something that had been nagging at my mind suddenly became quite clear.

That rope on John's scaffolding that I had glimpsed as I came up from the cellar—the end was not frayed or broken unevenly. It had been cut!

I pulled myself out of the chair and hurried from the room, leaving Freda in mid-sentence with her mouth hanging open. I went to the cellar door, switched on the dim light, and ran down the steps. I went around behind them, and then stopped dead.

The scaffolding was no longer there.

CHAPTER
6

I STOOD THERE FOR a moment, puzzled and uneasy, looking into the dusty space where the scaffolding had been. But there was no doubt about it. It had disappeared. I looked about the cellar a bit, but I was too conscious of the probable presence of rats and spiders to be at all thorough. I gave up the search before it was well started and went upstairs to find Berg.

I ran into Richard Jones in the kitchen. He stared at me and asked suspiciously, "Have you been messing around with my fire again?"

I said "No," impatiently and tried to brush past him.

He laid a restraining hand on my arm. "Then what were you doing in the cellar?"

"Looking for the scaffolding," I said wearily.

"What scaffolding?"

I pulled my arm away and tried to pass him again, but he stepped directly in front of me and repeated, "What scaffolding, Smithy?"

"The one John was standing on when he fell."

"John? But I thought he had slipped. I didn't know—"

"I'll speak very slowly and try to keep it to words of one syllable," I said bitterly. "John was standing on the scaffolding, and it broke. It was lying near him on the ground. Berg put it in the cellar, and now it's gone, and I want to find him and tell him about it."

He grinned at me oddly and stepped aside, and I hurried off, feeling that I had been rude, and excusing myself because I was so tired.

I could not find Berg at first, and then I remembered guiltily that he was sitting with John and that I had promised to have him relieved. I ran upstairs and went to the little sewing room at the end of the hall where they had put John. I knocked softly, and Berg opened the door. He looked tired, and I knew he thought he was going to be relieved. I felt sorry for him.

"Berg," I said, "didn't you put that scaffolding under the cellar stairs?"

"Yes. Why?"

"I went down there a little while ago, and it isn't there. Did you move it?"

"No," he said tiredly, "I haven't touched it. Are you sure it's gone?"

I nodded. "But that isn't all, Berg. I caught a glimpse of the rope, and it—it had been cut."

"Cut?" he repeated, staring at me.

"Yes, it was. I'm sure it was. I don't know what it means, but I wanted to look at it again."

He passed his hand through his hair almost fretfully. "What time is it?" he asked abruptly.

I glanced at my watch. "Ten o'clock," I said.

He came out of the room and closed the door quietly behind him. "Aunt Mabel isn't likely to wake up again, is she?"

I shook my head. "She's had a couple of sleeping tablets."

"Then there's no need to—to stay there any more." His voice broke, and he cleared his throat. "We'd better go down and see what's happened to that scaffolding."

We went to the cellar, discovered that the light was already on, and came upon Richard Jones, standing in the middle of the floor with the scaffolding in his hands.

"Where did you find it?" I asked breathlessly.

He looked up. "I'm not quite sure," he said slowly, "but I think it was in the excavation under that small porch at the side of the house."

He was covered with dust and cobwebs, but he seemed to be quite unconscious of his appearance. He went on gravely, "This looks bad, Berg. As far as I can make out, this rope has been cut all around leaving a small piece in the middle, which broke through, of course, as soon as there was any strain on it. The outer edges were evidently glued together. There are still particles of glue on them. Someone seems to have taken a lot of trouble over it."

He put the thing on the floor and mopped at his dusty face with his handkerchief.

"In short, Berg, if I were you, I'd phone the police."

Berg sat down on the cellar steps, as though the strength had suddenly gone out of his legs. "Oh, my God!" he said heavily. "My God! Who would *dare*—? Who'd *want* to? I can't believe it, Dick—I *can't.*"

I looked from one to the other and heard myself whisper, "You mean he was murdered?"

Richard put his handkerchief away and brushed at his coat with his hand.

"I may be mistaken," he said without conviction, "but it looks like it."

He picked up the scaffolding again, and we went upstairs. Berg phoned Dr. O'Beirne but was told by a female voice that he was out on a difficult case. She promised to leave a message telling him to call us but did not think he would be in before the early hours of the morning. Richard took the scaffolding to his bedroom, and I went up and looked in on Mrs. Ballinger and Rhynda. They were both sleeping, so I did not disturb them. As I walked down the hall, I heard Amy and Donald Tait arguing loudly in her room.

I opened the door, poked my head in, and asked them to be quiet, because I did not want Mrs. Ballinger or Rhynda to be awakened.

Donald said, "O.K.," and winked at me over Amy's head, but Amy turned on me and declared she'd wake up anyone she chose. She added a command that I stay out of her room except when I was cleaning it up.

I went off feeling well satisfied. I was used to her rudeness and no longer took much notice of it, but since she had suitably insulted me, I felt that there would no longer be any need to make her bed or tidy up her room.

I went down to the living room, where Freda and Rosalie were conversing earnestly. They broke off to give me a couple of polite nods as I sank into a chair and then went back to it again. I gathered that they were discussing funerals—what was desirable and what was not at the best-conducted affairs. It appeared that Rosalie's husband had had the ultimate in send-offs. Before Rosalie had half finished describing it I realized that it had been well worth Mr. Hannahs' while to die.

I relaxed in my chair and tried not to think of the disturbing things that were crowding my mind. My rest lasted for about five minutes, and then Amy and Donald walked in. Their argument had evidently ended amicably, for they were companionably arm in arm. They went to the fire, and Amy extended first one foot and then the other to the blaze and observed to no one in particular, "It's freezing in this damn house."

She looked down at me and added imperiously, "Leigh, we're hungry. Will you please get us some supper?"

"Not now," I said coldly, "nor at any other time whatsoever."

She pouted and said quite mildly, "Oh well, you don't have to be so cranky about it. Come on, Don, we'll see what's in the icebox."

Amy was always given to making the most ridiculous demands on people, but if she were firmly refused she usually took it as a matter of course. After she had left, I found that I was being applauded by Freda and Rosalie.

"I'm certainly glad that you put her in her place," Freda said earnestly. "*Dreadful* woman. She—well, really—" She put her head closer to Rosalie's and made some revelations about Amy that had my hair standing on end. If she were to be believed, Amy could be nothing less than Public Enemy Number One.

I did not take much notice of it all, because I knew that Freda violently disliked Amy and, in fact, had threatened her only yesterday. Rosalie did not seem much impressed by Freda's lurid tales, either. She shook her head at intervals and clicked her tongue, and when she could decently break in she started telling about a friend of hers who did bigger and worse things than Amy.

I fell asleep in the midst of this recital and must have slept soundly for quite a long time. I woke up feeling chilly and stiff and very uncomfortable, to find that the fire was nearly out and I was alone in the room. I lay still for a moment and quite without my own volition, my mind observed chattily, "There is probably a murderer just outside the door of this room, and he is coming in to kill I me."

I shivered, pulled myself together, and stood up. I saw that it was a quarter past twelve, and I began hastily to tidy up the room. The house was very quiet, and it began to get on my nerves. I started to hurry with my work until I was simply flying about the room. I had nearly finished when the heavy silence was broken by the sound of clear, slow footsteps. I stopped dead, with a dirty ashtray in each hand, and stared at the doorway. I was so frightened that I could feel my toes curl.

However, it turned out to be nothing more alarming than Richard Jones walking carefully because he had a loaded tray in his hands. I nearly threw the ashtrays at him in reaction from my scare. He set the tray on a low table and put another log on the fire. He turned to me then, and relieved me of the two ashtrays.

"Smithy," he said gloomily, "I'm worried about you, and I'm worried for your future husband. This passion for midnight housework seems to be growing on you, and no man will stand for being turned out of his bed in the early hours of the morning so that you may change the sheets. Sit down."

I sat, and started to explain defensively, "But it must be done now, because tomorrow—"

"My dear Smithy," he interrupted smoothly, "all addicts have perfect explanations for having just one more. Pour the coffee, will you? They've all gone to bed, and I prepared this bit of supper with my own hands for you and myself. Incidentally, our pal Amy left the kitchen in a muck that would be offensive to a pig of the better type."

I started in hungrily on the supper and said of Amy, "She always does. But Doris will spit in her coffee tomorrow morning, so it all works out in the end."

We had almost finished before I realized that we were eating Mrs. Ballinger's breakfast herring. I dropped my fork and stared at him in consternation.

He raised his eyebrows in a query. "What is it? Did you forget to wax the floors?"

"Richard," I said hollowly, "I'll be fired, and you'll be had up for stealing. This is Mrs. Ballinger's breakfast."

"I don't think she'd care for it now," he said cheerfully. "And don't worry about her. I'll make her a pfannkuchen in the morning that will drive all thought of herring from her mind."

"What's a pfannkuchen?"

"You wouldn't know," he said loftily. "Finish up your supper. It's late."

He carried the tray back to the kitchen and then went down to the cellar to attend to the furnace while I finished putting the room in order.

The place seemed to get black and frightening again when I was left alone in it. I became conscious of the wind howling outside, and I noticed that the heavy portieres hanging in the doorway were swaying slightly.

We went upstairs, and I said good night to Richard in the hall and hurried into my room. I closed the door firmly and began to think about John immediately, although I did not want to. He had been so quiet and so nice, it seemed impossible that anybody could have hated him enough to want to kill him.

I was a bit worried because we had disregarded Mrs. Ballinger's orders to have someone sit with the body, but it had seemed an impossible thing to ask of anyone. I began to wonder whether Berg had gone back there, and at last I opened my door and looked down the hall. It was quite dark—no light coming from under the door of the sewing room—so I decided that Berg had gone to bed, since it was unlikely that he would be sitting there in the dark. I locked my door and got into bed myself.

I was wide awake at once. I turned restlessly for some time and blamed it on the two cups of coffee and the naps I had had. And then the shutter began to bang. I knew it was the one on the sewing-room window because it had worked loose once before. I told myself fiercely that I was not going down the dark hall and into that death room to fix it, and I lay for some time, clinging to this determination and waiting nervously for each successive bang.

I was not able to stand it for long. It seemed to me that the crashes grew louder each time, and that they must soon wake the entire household. I gritted my teeth, got out of bed and into a dressing gown and slippers, and went out into the hall.

I felt an instant surge of relief. There was a thin stream of light coming from under the sewing-room door now, and I was sure that one of the men had heard the noise and had gone to fix it. I felt that my knowledge of the intricacies of that shutter might be useful, so I went confidently down the hall. I had my hand on the knob of the door when Mrs. Ballinger's story of how the Ballinger corpses walked if they were left alone flashed into my mind.

I squared my shoulders against the feeling of horror that thrilled over me and resolutely opened the door.

The room was well-lighted and empty—except for John. And he was sitting on a chair, facing me, with his eyes wide open and his mouth stretched in an insane grin.

CHAPTER
7

I BACKED AWAY SLOWLY from the door, and the dead eyes seemed to follow me. And then I started to scream. I believe I screamed steadily until I became conscious of two indistinct figures, one on each side of me. I pointed to the sewing-room door with a shaking finger, and one of them went in. The other held me up while I sobbed on his chest.

The man at the door came out and shut it, and then someone put the hall light on. I could hear them come out of their rooms and gather around, talking excitedly. I still clung, trembling, to whoever was supporting me, but I had come out of my dazed state sufficiently to notice that the chest on which I had been dropping tears was handsomely garbed in a dressing gown of heavy, royal blue silk.

I was presently yanked away from this haven by Berg, who took over the job of holding me up. I discovered then that the royal blue enveloped Donald Tait and that Amy was staring at me with evil in her eyes.

They were all there except Doris, who seemed able to sleep through anything. Mrs. Ballinger kept demanding to see John and wanted to know who had been sitting with him, and why I had screamed.

Berg said to me, "Tell us what happened," and three times I opened my mouth to explain, but they were all talking at once and I could not make myself heard.

Mrs. Ballinger got a bit hysterical at last and shouted out that she was going to see for herself. She made a determined effort to enter the sewing room and was as firmly restrained by Richard Jones, who thereupon loudly demanded silence. Rather surprisingly, he got it. They all turned and looked at him, and he said briefly, "What happened is simply this. Leigh went into the room for something and found John siting on a chair instead of being on the bed."

I nodded and found, to my annoyance, that I was hard put to it to keep from breaking into tears again.

"What did she go in for?" Amy asked.

I explained about the shutter and added rather resentfully, "It was banging frightfully."

Freda backed me up. "I heard it myself," she said, "only I didn't know where it was coming from."

Mrs. Ballinger suddenly caught on to the fact that John had been left alone against her express order and became hysterical again. Freda and I took her in hand, while Richard and Berg went to the telephone to try and get in touch with Dr. O'Beirne. We got Mrs. Ballinger to bed and induced her to take another sleeping tablet, and after a while she became quiet and went to sleep. We left her and went off to find the rest of them congregated in Rhynda's room. Freda sat down in a straight chair and folded her hands, and I found a seat on a low footstool.

Berg was speaking. He said, "We ought to try and find out about this—do a little investigating, here and now. Dr. O'Beirne will be here sometime tonight, and we ought to get to the bottom of it before he comes. It might save a lot of unpleasantness."

"We ought to send for the police," I said.

My remark dropped into a pool of silence, and I received one or two glances of faint hostility. After a moment, Rhynda said coldly, "I don't think that's at all necessary. Dr. O'Beirne is the coroner, and if we notify him that should be enough."

Berg looked around at us all and made an earnest appeal. "If any of you did it for a joke, please say so. We won't take it badly. But, I—we *must* know. If you will only admit it, we'll put him back on the bed and say no more about it."

No one answered this plea, but after a moment of silence Freda said in a low, strained voice, "It's no use. Nobody moved him. You know this house, and a Ballinger—somebody should have watched him."

"That's nonsense!" Rhynda said sharply. Her face was white and drawn, and she picked constantly and aimlessly at the bedclothes. "It's stupid to talk like that, Freda. Of course somebody moved John, and I add my plea to Berg's—please tell us about it. We'll put John back and simply forget it."

"Why not put him back, anyway?" said Amy.

I expected them all to jump on her, but instead there was a faintly embarrassed silence.

"Let's put it to a vote," Rosalie suggested tentatively.

There was another uneasy silence, and then Richard Jones stood up abruptly. "Sorry if I stand alone on this, but I'm afraid there's nothing doing. If you put him back, I'll tell O'Beirne about it."

"He's right," Berg said flatly. "It wouldn't be any use. It's stupid."

"I think you'd all better go back to bed," Richard suggested. "Berg and I will attend to things."

Nobody wanted to go much, but we had nothing else to do so we wandered off. Freda came into my room through the connecting door that led to hers. She said she was too frightened to stay in her own room, and she huddled into a small, armless rocking chair and gazed drearily out of the little bay window at the foot of my bed.

I stretched out on the bed, but I could not sleep. I kept wondering if John had been alive after all and had got himself up. I closed my eyes but could not forget his bloodstained face, and after a while I began to have spasms of trembling that I could not control.

From the foot of the bed Freda said suddenly, "Don't! Stop shuddering like that. I can't stand it!"

She started to cry, and I pulled myself out of bed and went and patted her a bit and tried to comfort her. I knew she had been very fond of John. There was no doubt on that score.

Her gasping sobs eased off presently, and she told me to go back to bed. I climbed in, and after a short silence, she said unexpectedly, "Leigh, I know who moved John. But I can't think why. I've tried to puzzle it out until my head is spinning with it—and there simply isn't any answer."

Her voice rose until she was almost shouting, and I said sharply, "Be quiet! You're making too much noise!"

She dropped her head against the back of the rocker and was

silent. I hated to stir her up again, but I felt that I could not let the thing go by. It was important to us all to know who had moved John, and I frankly admitted to myself my own personal curiosity. I gave her a minute or two, and then I asked her, quietly, who had done it and how she knew about it.

"I saw," she replied simply.

I sat up in bed, in my eagerness. "Then, Freda, you *must* tell us. You must. If you won't talk to anyone else, tell Dr. O'Beirne. It's so desperately important."

"No, I won't," she said flatly. "Not until I'm good and ready, anyway."

I dropped back on my pillow again and closed my eyes. I knew Freda. If she had made up her mind not to tell, then nothing on earth could make her. I wondered what Amy had done to anger her and decided to risk a question about it. I was too tired to think up any diplomatic approach, so asked bluntly, "What has Amy done to you, Freda?"

I heard the rocker creak, as though she had made a sudden movement, and she said, in a strained unnatural voice, "Why, what do you mean?"

I tried to be casual. "Oh, I know there's something. I wondered what it could be."

"How did you know?" she asked suspiciously.

"I could see it."

She began to rock in an agitated fashion. After a moment she said with subdued violence, "Well, you're right. She has done something, and it's so abominable that this time at least she's going to be paid out for it." She was quite vicious about it, and I decided, without sorrow, that Amy was due for retaliation in some distinctly unpleasant form.

"But what was it she did to you?" I asked curiously.

I believe she was going to tell me. She stopped rocking and cleared her throat, and just at that minute we heard the voices of Richard, Berg, and Dr. O'Beirne as they mounted the stairs.

We both scrambled up and went out into the hall to see the men just disappearing into the sewing room. Freda stopped and suddenly clutched at my arm.

"Don't tell them," she said fiercely. "You're not to tell them that I know who moved him. I'll tell them myself, but first there's something I must do. Say you won't tell them, please, Leigh. I promise, on my word of honor, that I'll go to them myself after I've done what I have to do."

I promised reluctantly and tried again to get her to tell me what she knew, but she closed her mouth in a thin, straight line and said "No, not yet."

The others began to drift out of their bedrooms, and presently we were all congregated near the door of the sewing room, with the exception of Mrs. Ballinger, who continued to sleep under the influence of her tablets.

It was just four o'clock.

Dr. O'Beirne and the others came out of the sewing room, and the doctor asked about the undertaker. I said I expected him in the morning, and he shook his head in an annoyed fashion and declared that he should have come last night.

Rhynda spoke up suddenly. "Was he dead?" she asked painfully. "I mean, the first time? Could he—could he have moved himself?"

"Definitely not," O'Beirne said shortly.

He asked us if we would come downstairs, because he wanted to question us. He said it could wait if we wanted to go back and sleep, but we all followed him down almost eagerly.

Richard went down to jack up the furnace, and Berg began to build a fire in the open fireplace. When he had got it started, he said to me, with something of his old wheedling charm, "Smithy, would you be a boy scout and make us some coffee? This may be a long session, and we're all out on our feet. I know you are too, but you're the only one can make coffee that isn't garbage."

It was always nearly impossible to resist Berg, so I agreed and asked the others to say which of them wanted coffee. There was not one dissenting voice, and as I turned to go Amy added, "Personally, I feel like a poached egg."

"Not at all surprising," I said coldly, "because you look like one, too."

I hurried off before she could think of the right answering insult.

Dr. O'Beirne did not keep us very long, after all. Richard showed him the scaffolding, and he wanted to know why it had not been mentioned on his first visit. Richard, Berg and I had quite a bit of trouble convincing him of our innocence in the matter, and I think I was under separate and particular suspicion because of my subsequent nocturnal trip to the sewing room. He listened to my story in silence and then turned away and went to the telephone, where he had a few words with the local police.

He told us all to go back to bed after that. We trailed off upstairs, and Freda came back into my room with me. I did not feel sleepy and was about to try and pump her again when she peered out into the hall and reported that O'Beirne was seated on a chair directly in front of the sewing room door. She declared that everything would be all right now and that she wasn't frightened any more, and she went off to her own room.

I decided to have a look too, and I tiptoed to the door and opened it to a crack. The chair stood in front of the sewing room door, but Dr. O'Beirne was not there. I opened the door a little wider and caught a glimpse of him disappearing into the bathroom.

I started to close the door, when a faint sound caught my attention and I looked out again.

Freda was walking swiftly down the corridor. As I stared at her with my mouth open, she went straight to the door of Donald Tait's room and, without knocking, opened it and went in.

CHAPTER
8

I STOOD STARING FOR some time after the door had closed. There was no doubt about the room. It belonged to Donald Tait, and there was no doubt that Freda had walked straight in without so much as a preliminary tap to announce herself.

Dr. O'Beirne came out of the bathroom just then, so I closed my door and went back to bed.

I was completely puzzled. There did not seem to be any reasonable explanation. I wondered how Freda was going to get back to her own room. She could not possibly make it without being seen by Dr. O'Beirne, and it seemed to me that the only alternative was to stay in Donald's room all night. I decided at last that I did not really care and dozed off into a badly needed sleep.

Doris woke me at eight o'clock and announced, with arms akimbo, that the cop was here.

"What cop?" I asked sleepily.

"The town cop."

"Is there only one?" I asked. "What do they do with the taxpayers' money?"

"There's a couple others," said Doris, "but Joe's the boss, see?"

"Yes," I said. "I see."

"He's my cousin," she admitted reluctantly, "but I ain't to be blamed for that. He's a nagger and a nosy parker. He's been naggin' me all morning to get you folks up so he can ask you a lot of questions that ain't, rightly speaking, none of his business."

I yawned and dragged myself away from the pillow. "I'll get dressed right away, Doris."

"Better hurry," she agreed comfortably. "I routed all the others out first, and they're all dressin'. Breakfast's at eight-thirty sharp."

She turned to go, and I called after her, "Wait a minute. Was Freda in her own bedroom when you went in to wake her up?"

She looked at me in blank surprise that changed slowly to a scornful chuckle. "Sure. You'll never find that one in any bed but her own, poor soul," she observed and closed the door firmly behind her.

I knew there would be no chance at the bathroom, with them all dressing at once, so I threw my clothes on and went down to wash at the kitchen sink.

Joe was seated at the kitchen table downing a hearty breakfast. He was a round fat fellow with very little hair on his head and a sour expression on his face. Nearly all the food that was to have been our breakfast that morning was piled on the plate in front of him. There were three eggs, a heaping mound of bacon, and six pieces of toast. I knew that we had been due for half an egg each, scrambled and proportioned evenly, and one strip of bacon each, and I looked at Joe and his steadily champing jaws with a feeling of sheer panic.

Doris came over to me and jerked a thumb at her relative. "I had to feed him. He's been nosing around since twenty of six , and his mother would put it all over town about me if I didn't do it decent."

I thought Joe might take offense at this frank statement, but he continued to shovel food into his mouth as though neither of us existed.

"Not only that," Doris continued, "but I had to dish up breakfast to the Doc—that feller, O'Beirne—and he's as greedy as Joe here, so that took three more eggs and the rest of the bacon."

"My God!" I said hollowly. "What are we going to do?"

She shrugged and turned back to the stove. "Pancakes," she said briefly.

As I went off, I heard Joe say, "Which one is that?"

I plunged into the housework and got through quite a lot of dusting and sweeping before the breakfast bell rang. It went off at nine o'clock, exactly, and I knew that Doris had planned it for nine and had told everyone half past eight so that they would be down in time.

I had hoped that Mrs. Ballinger might sleep late, but to my disappointment she sailed into the dining room with the rest of them. I knew it meant an immediate explanation regarding the pancakes.

Everyone seemed quiet that morning and vaguely uneasy, with the exception of Mrs. Ballinger, who talked too much. She started off by saying icily, "And what, may I ask, has been done with bacon and eggs this morning?"

I was too tired for any more diplomacy where she was concerned. I said shortly, "They were fed to Dr. O'Beirne and Joe, the cop."

Richard raised his head and looked at me. "Joe, the cop?"

"In the kitchen," I explained briefly. "He's number one boy on the town police force. The force consists of three in all, but the other two are used only for parades and to help old ladies across the street, because Joe can do it all with one hand tied behind him."

"Leigh," said Mrs. Ballinger, in a deadly voice, "will you stop that stupid nonsense, so that I can get a word in edgewise at my own table? You are to tell Doris that she is not to give those people another mouthful! I don't see that I should be called upon to feed them, and I won't have it. It's bad enough for them to trample through my house and upset everything!"

She continued to whine shrilly through the entire meal. When we had finished, we went to the living room, and she gave voice to a fresh complaint. She looked around her, sniffed, and remarked that the room was not particularly well-cleaned.

I was so angry that I dared not answer her. I felt that I had done everything humanly possible to keep the house fairly presentable.

Richard said easily, "It's nice and tidy, but of course it could do with a bit more spit and polish. But I don't believe anyone would dream of blaming you, Mrs. Ballinger, after what you have been through. Leigh, of course, has been doing more than her share, and

I'm sure that she'll continue to try and make up for what you are unable to do while you're still so upset."

I smiled at him gratefully. Mrs. Ballinger gave him a long, cold stare. She knew impertinence even when it was garnished, but she eventually decided to let it pass.

"I don't quite understand what that policeman is doing here," she said instead. "Will someone kindly tell me?"

Apparently no one would. I was watching Richard and Rhynda, who were deep in a low-toned conversation—there seemed to be no doubt that they knew each other very well—and I was busy trying to explain to myself an inexplicable feeling of pique.

Freda and Rosalie sat together on a couch and talked desultorily. I looked at Freda at regular intervals, to see if she were exchanging glances of any sort with Donald Tait, but there was nothing. Her manner to him was as to a stranger whom she hardly knew. Amy, of course, was hanging on to his arm. Berg sat beside me, and it suddenly occurred to me that he had been paying me a little attention just recently. I felt oddly pleased about it.

I think Mrs. Ballinger was about to make a second demand for an explanation when Policeman Joe appeared suddenly in the doorway. He stood looking us over impersonally and picking his teeth. Mrs. Ballinger turned a mottled red with indignation at the sight of this intruder calmly picking out of his teeth her good bacon and eggs.

"What are you doing here, my man?" she asked sharply. "If you are a friend of Doris's, you must confine yourself to the kitchen."

It was obvious that she knew perfectly well who he was. He ignored her, and after completing his casual survey of us, suddenly waved his arm in a large gesture and shouted, "Everyone be seated."

We all came to attention with startling promptness. There is nothing like a loud raucous voice to get a crowd under control.

He pinned us down with his eyes, and while we sat silent, he stood rocking backwards and forwards on his heels and toes, hands in his pockets and the toothpick sprouting from one corner of his mouth. When he was good and ready, he started to speak.

"Someone," he rumbled, "cut the rope on Mr. John Ballinger's scaffolding and glued it together again, and someone moved his dead body to a chair last night. One of youse."

We stared at him in fearful silence.

"Doc O'Beirne has taken the body for an autopsy," he continued, "and while I'm waiting for the report, I'm going to question you."

"Youse," Berg corrected with dignity. "Plural, you know."

Mrs. Ballinger said shrilly, "By what right?"

"It's a matter of law and order," Joe deigned to explain. "When it's a case of murder, I have to investigate. That's what they pay me for."

"I'm glad to know that," Berg said amiably. "I'd been wondering."

Mrs. Ballinger rose up from her seat and stared before her like a blind person.

"John," she whispered. "Murdered! Oh no! That isn't possible!"

The rest of us watched her uncomfortably. We all knew by this time that John had been murdered, or at least we were pretty sure of it.

I wondered why they bothered to do an autopsy. It seemed quite unnecessary to me. After all, they knew why he died—he had hit the ground too hard.

I found myself shaking with silent laughter at this point and realized with a shock that I was hysterical. I rested my head against the back of my chair, closed my eyes, and tried to think of ordinary, everyday things.

Joe started to ask his questions, but I concentrated fiercely on whether I would buy a pink collar or a white collar for one of my dresses. I never decided it, for I heard Freda say clearly, "I know Amy cut that rope, because I saw her do it."

CHAPTER
9

THE STUNNED SILENCE that followed Freda's declaration did not last very long, and it was succeeded by a miniature riot.

When Amy found her voice, she used it long and shrilly, and all the other people who were trying to get a word in were merely chorus. She shouted at Freda, berated us in general, and then blazed at Freda again.

"How dare you tell a wicked lie like that?" she stormed. "Just for the sake of revenge—don't think I don't know, you vicious shrew!

Joe yelled, "Miss Perrin!"

She abandoned Freda and turned on him.

"Don't you start trying to ask me any questions! I won't have anything to do with it, and I won't be made the victim of a sour woman. I'm through with the whole business. I'm going home at once, Donald!"

Donald stirred and said uncomfortably, "You can't go now, Amy."

She flounced out of the room, and Joe watched her stolidly, his eyes speculative and the toothpick still tucked into the corner of his mouth. He made no effort to stop her, but when Donald started after her, he waved him back with a peremptory gesture.

"Just a minute, young feller, I want to talk to you. Are you engaged to that dame?"

Donald colored and said, "No," with faint emphasis.

"Just the boyfriend?" Joe suggested frankly.

Donald hesitated, glanced around uneasily, and gave a brief nod. Freda flicked her eyes at him and said suddenly and tonelessly, "He has no right. He's married."

Donald shot her a malevolent glance and said irritably, "Good Lord! Amy knows I'm married—my wife knows that I go out with Amy occasionally. We are just friends."

Berg nudged me and murmured, "How about being just friends with me, Smithy?" and I choked down a desire to giggle.

Mrs. Ballinger had assumed an expression of high moral indignation. I could see that she thought she had found an excellent opportunity to get rid of some of her unwanted guests. She dove right in.

"How dare you, a married man, accompany a young girl like Amy to a houseparty! I won't have anything of the sort under my roof. You'll have to leave at once."

Donald bowed, murmured, "Glad to," and turned towards the door, but Joe stopped him.

"No soap, brother," said the Law. "Nobody's leavin' here until I get this thing cleared up."

He suddenly turned on his heel and left the room, and almost immediately there were sounds of battle. He apparently won out in the fracas and returned presently with Amy in tow. She wore a hat and coat and clutched a purse that did not match either and she had no gloves or suitcase. She must have come down the stairs quietly, for I had not heard her, and I decided that Joe took in more than I'd given him credit for.

Amy's belligerence had died down and she looked definitely frightened. I knew that she did not frighten easily, and I wondered if Freda's bald statement could possibly be true. And if so, why? It did not seem to make much sense. I think Joe figured that he had broken the back of the morning's work by subduing Amy, and he plunged into the investigation without further ado. He brooked no fooling when he asked a question. You answered him, or else.

We were all putty in his hands but Freda. He stubbed his toe on Freda. She refused steadily to say anything more about Amy or about anything else. She merely passed the remark that Joe could put her on the torture rack but she still would say no more than she had.

Joe, the iron man, began almost to plead. "Just a few little details, lady," he wheedled. But Freda set her mouth obstinately, and he was forced to give up. He turned his attention to Amy.

Amy had pulled herself together. She spoke clearly and with something of her usual imperious manner. She denied emphatically any knowledge of John's scaffolding. She had not known that he used one and was only vaguely aware, in any case, that he had intended repairing the roof. She turned on Freda at last and said haughtily, "You had better prove your statement pretty quickly, or I shall sue you for libel."

Berg chuckled quietly, and I giggled into my handkerchief. Freda ignored everyone and continued to sit like a graven image.

Joe gave indication that he had finished with Amy, and she swept over to a chair beside Donald and took one of his hands in her own. He tried quietly to disengage himself, but she hung on tightly.

Mrs. Ballinger reared her head and leaned forward excitedly in her chair. "Amy, I will not tolerate your sitting there and brazenly holding that man's hand. My only excuse for you is that you probably do not know that he is married."

Amy looked up quickly and frowned in annoyance. "Who told you that?"

Joe cleared his throat. "You ladies'll have to quit scrappin'. I can't hang around here all day—I've gotta find out what happened."

He bore down on us like a steamroller then. He was an inexhaustible questioner, and he insisted on having your entire life's history before he came down to what actually happened. As time went on, I found that I was learning more about the people around me than I had ever known before.

I believe I was under fire for a longer time than any one of the others, and the only memory I had of it afterwards was that I had told all about my affair with Bill Turner. I had practically forgotten Bill, but by the time I had finished telling it, it sounded as though he had been my grand passion, and since he had gone out of my life I was merely waiting for merciful death to end my suffering.

Joe had prefaced the inquisition by explaining, "I like to know the whole dope—everything—and then I can tell better if a person is lying or not."

I reflected bitterly that Joe practically forced you to lie. Bill Turner had been nothing more than an escort to me, but as the appalling saga went on, I found myself the target of a good many sympathetic and pitying glances.

Joe plowed on steadily, and I began to wonder if I could control my fury sufficiently to keep from slapping his face. When he finished at last I realized that I had scarcely heard the last few questions as I had been too busy mentally rehearsing a vigorous denial to the others of all the lies he had made me tell about my private life.

I had been the last to be turned inside out, and Joe departed immediately afterwards. The others scattered as soon as his back was well-turned, and I was left alone with a lot of housework staring me in the face. I sat for a while looking moodily at the dust and disorder,and had nearly prodded myself into getting up and at it when Richard came back.

He wore an evil smile, and he said in a hushed voice, "I'm so sorry, Miss Smith. I didn't know. You should have given us a hint."

"Shut up!" I said furiously.

"I'd like to have a shot at mending the broken places," he went on. "In other words, I want to make a date with you."

I looked at him suspiciously. It had been a long time since I'd had a date. "Where do you want to take me—the opera, perhaps?"

He shook his head. "Opera should always be heard but not seen, and in my case, I thought to work up slowly. How about starting off with a ride in my car this afternoon?"

"That would be delightful, Mr. Jones," I murmured. "Perhaps we could be a wee bit dashing and stop in at the village drugstore for a soda."

"Don't give me any of your solid gold sarcasm, Smithy," he said sternly. "And now for the housework. We have half an hour before lunch in which to get all the dust swept under the rugs and the house generally tidy."

"Don't be ridiculous," I protested. "We couldn't possibly—"

"Stop wasting time," said Richard.

The room was done in exactly five minutes, and certainly my help was negligible. I was too weak with laughter to do much.

He simply threw everything in sight into drawers and out of the window. He dusted with one sweep of his arms and ran the mop around whatever pieces of floor were showing. We went to the dining room next, and I began to get into the spirit of the thing, with the result that the entire lower floor was done in fifteen minutes.

We went upstairs then. Richard's room, my room, Berg's room, and the bathroom, all came under the same treatment. We paused, at last, at the door of the sewing room, where John had been. I did not want to go in and was glad when Richard turned away.

"When is the funeral?" he asked.

"Tomorrow," I said soberly.

He looked up and down the hall. "Any more rooms?"

I shook my head. "Just Amy's and Donald Tait's, and I'm not going to do them any more."

"No shirking," he said reprovingly. "Come on."

He went to Amy's door, knocked loudly, and without waiting walked straight in. I heard her give a little shriek and then saw that she was in panties and brassiere.

He took no notice of her beyond brushing her aside while he made the bed with a few vigorous strokes while she began to yell at us to get out.

Her room, as usual, was in a violent mess, with her clothes all over the place. Richard stuffed them all under the bed and turned a deaf ear to her shrieked invectives. He climaxed his performance by throwing her magazines and a box of chocolates out of the window, after which we left as abruptly as we had come.

Amy followed us out into the hall, shrilling abuse.

Unexpectedly we ran into Mrs. Ballinger, and the shock and outrage on her face brought us to a standstill. Amy continued to complain in a high voice and her panties.

"Amy!" said Mrs. Ballinger, in a truly terrible voice. "Go back to your room at once and put on some decent clothing!"

Amy gave her a black look, swung herself about, and slammed the door behind her.

I was dealt with next. "Leigh Smith, you are discharged. Leave at once. All this noise and levity—disgraceful! With John not yet in his grave."

She sailed off, and I looked helplessly at Richard and Berg, who had come up to find out what the rumpus was about. Berg patted my shoulder.

"Never you mind, Smithy. Dick or I will marry you, and you can have a nice easy time cooking and washing for your living."

"Very helpful," I said bitterly. "I'll go and pack, while you toss for me."

I walked off towards my room. I was furious with Mrs. Ballinger, and I wanted to get out of her house as soon as was humanly possible. I felt that it would be a relief not to have to spend another night in the frightening place. Richard came after me and laid a detaining hand on my arm.

"I don't think they'll allow you to go, Leigh. Hadn't you better find out about it, before you pack?"

Before I could reply, Rosalie Hannahs came racing down the hall.

"Miss Smith, Miss Smith," she called excitedly. "Come quickly. Rhynda is having hysterics. She keeps crying out that she is going to have a baby."

CHAPTER
10

I FORGOT ABOUT HAVING been fired and hurried after Rosalie downstairs to the living room.

We found Rhynda lying on a couch, crying and laughing and gasping at intervals that she was going to have a baby, and it was not fair. Richard brushed me aside and leaned over her. It took him two minutes to shut her up, and then he lifted her and carried her upstairs to her bedroom.

She clung to him, whimpering a little. "Stay with me, Dick. Don't leave me alone. I don't want to be alone."

He mixed up some sort of a concoction in a glass and made her drink it and then sat down beside her and stroked her hair, or something. I went off feeling inexplicably annoyed. But I could not help being sorry for Rhynda. If it was true that she was pregnant, it was rather hard luck.

The luncheon gong had gone off in the midst of the row, so I went down to the dining room. Rosalie was telling them all about Rhynda, and Amy was complaining to Mrs. Ballinger in a steady stream about the way her room had been cleaned. The noise was pretty bad, and I slid into a chair and attacked my almost empty plate with the idea of getting finished and away again as soon as I decently could. But Mrs. Ballinger had evidently decided on a family council, for she suddenly rapped on the table and demanded quiet.

"There are certain things we must talk over," she announced importantly.

"Then, perhaps, I had better go," I said coldly.

She looked me over. "No. I believe you know as much about this as the rest of us, if not more."

My dignity urged me to walk out on her, but my curiosity was too strong. I froze my face and remained where I was.

"They tell me," she began pompously, "that John was murdered—my poor John! And I won't rest—I *cannot* rest until the creature who did it is brought to justice."

Nobody said anything. We just sat and waited. Mrs. Ballinger had opened her mouth to proceed when Richard walked into the room and took his place at the table. There was practically no food left by that time, so he took Freda's plate, which seemed hardly to have been touched. He started to eat, and everybody watched him in silence, until he became conscious of it.

He looked up and raised his eyebrows. "Please!" he said with dignity. "I am not on exhibition. Either talk or leave the table."

Mrs. Ballinger frowned at him. "We are waiting for you to finish, young man, so that we can hold a conference." She glanced around the table. "I think we can start now, anyway, if he'll try to eat a little more quietly."

"May I trouble someone for the celery?" said Richard politely.

She stared at him for a moment and said, "Very impertinent. Now! As I see it, Freda accuses Amy of having deliberately murdered John. It that right, Freda?"

Freda and Amy both started up together, but she cut them off short.

"Be quiet, Amy," she said sharply. "We'll hear from you later. Now, Freda—please explain."

Freda was pink with indignation. "I never accused her of murdering John. I did no such thing at any time, and you have no right to put words in my mouth."

Mrs. Ballinger blinked. "But you said you saw Amy cut the rope on that scaffolding, and then glue it together again."

"I said nothing about seeing her glue it together. I merely saw her cut the rope."

"Where?" said Richard suddenly.

Freda turned her head quickly and looked at him. She appeared to be distinctly uneasy. "What do you mean, 'where'?" she asked defensively.

"Freda," Berg said gently, "tell us where Amy was when you saw her cutting that rope."

"She was in her own room."

Amy got her say in, at this point.

"You crazy idiot!" she shouted. "That was the rope off my suitcase. One of the locks broke at the last minute, and I tied the cord around as I was rushing out. I was cutting it off my bag so that I could get the damn thing open."

"Is that true, Freda?" Mrs. Ballinger demanded sternly.

Freda had turned sullen. "All I know is that she was cutting a rope in her room that looked very like the rope on John's scaffolding." She got up and walked off, as she always did when things got too hot for her.

"The nerve of her," Amy said. "Accusing me of a thing like that!"

Donald Tait muttered, "Hush, Amy. Be quiet," and she flared shrilly, "I will not be quiet."

Mrs. Ballinger rose from the table. "Leigh, I want you in the den. We must make arrangements about tomorrow. There's a lot to do."

"You fired Leigh," Richard reminded her. "She has time only to pack and make her train. You'll have to get Amy to help you."

He took my arm and marched me quickly out of the room while Mrs. Ballinger snorted angrily and Amy refused, point-blank, to have anything to do with any arrangements.

"Get your bonnet and dolman," said Richard, "and meet me out in the front. I'll bring the car around. And hurry—before she rehires you."

I ran upstairs and marveled that I should be fairly glowing at the prospect of an automobile ride on a cold day when I had always regarded a car solely as a means of transportation. I ran into Rhynda in the upper hall and tried to get by with a brief smile.

"Leigh! Wait a minute! For heaven's sake. Where is everybody?" she demanded crossly.

"Just finished lunch," I said, and added politely, "How are you feeling?"

She brushed it aside impatiently. "Oh, I'm all right. Where's Richard?"

I hesitated and then said reluctantly, "He's—he's outside."

"Where? What is he doing?"

"He's getting his car out," I explained, still reluctant. "He's taking me for a ride."

She looked me over coldly and decided suddenly, "I'll go too. I need the air."

There didn't seem to be anything to say to that, so I went to my room. I powdered up a bit, got my coat and hat, and hurried downstairs. Rhynda had beaten me to it, though. When I walked out onto the veranda, I saw that she was already established in the front seat of Richard's car. I thought his manner was a bit cool and formal as he handed me into the back seat, and I began to feel like an intruder. I suddenly wished to God that I had stayed at home.

I might just as well have, for the ride was a complete washout. Rhynda had the heater on in the front seat, but I was cold in the back. Not one of us seemed to have anything to say, and I began to wonder why we were driving around aimlessly in the midst of winter.

We had not been on the way more than fifteen minutes when Rhynda turned to me and asked if I would mind if they dropped me at the drugstore for a soda, as she wanted to talk to Richard alone.

"I don't care for sodas," I said coldly, "but if you'll just drop me back at the house, I shall be pleased to get out and let you go on with your drive."

Neither of them said anything, but Richard turned the car around with vicious jerks of the wheel and raced back to the house with unnecessary speed. He stopped at the door, got out, and opened up for me.

"Thanks for the date," I said stiffly.

He bowed and murmured, "Pleasure," after which he got back into the car, slammed the door, and drove off furiously.

I went into the house and came upon Mrs. Ballinger in the hall.

"Where is Rhynda?" she demanded excitedly. "How could you do such a senseless thing as to take her out into the cold, when she has been so ill?"

"I am not Rhynda's nursemaid, Mrs. Ballinger," I pointed out and passed her by.

"Whatever in the world has come over you, Leigh?" she wailed after me. "You used to be such a nice obliging girl. I can't make you out."

I left her to wrestle with the problem and went to my own room. I closed the door firmly, stretched out on the bed, and lit a cigarette. I was angry at Rhynda for having spoiled my outing, and I was angry at Richard for letting her.

"I suppose she'll marry him now that John's gone," I thought, and was suddenly in a cold fury that I could not account for. It was not, I told myself haughtily, that I cared anything for Richard Jones. Oh no, oh no, no, no.

There was a tap on the door, which was followed by Berg. He came in and seated himself on the small rocker and stared out of the window without seeming to have much to say. I was not in a chatty mood, myself, so I lay quietly and studied his profile. I came to the conclusion that it was pretty good. His chin was strong and showed no signs, as yet, of repeating itself—straight nose, humorous mouth. His hair had started to recede at the temples, but it was only the beginning and merely made him look more intellectual.

He spoke suddenly. "Leigh—they're a bunch of crazy fools in this house, and I think it's up to you and me to get to the bottom of it all. Joe's all right, I suppose, but he's only a hick cop. He'll never dig up anything but the skeletons in our closets."

"He'll furnish you with a skeleton if you don't happen to have one," I said bitterly. "Anyway, what can we do? We don't know any more about it than Joe does, and he's paid to try and dig out the truth. Maybe we wouldn't like the truth if we found it. Perhaps it would be better if it never came to light."

He set his jaw and said stubbornly, "Someone is going to pay for what happened to John."

I closed my eyes and let it go at that, because I did not want to talk about it. He sat on for a while, staring out of the window, and then he stood up abruptly.

"Do you know where Richard is?"

"Yes," I said acidly. "He's taking Rhynda for a ride in his car."

"Taking Rhynda for a ride?" he repeated vaguely and wandered out.I turned over and made myself comfortable for the nap I felt coming on.

I slept for some time, and when I woke up again it was almost dark, and the wind was howling dismally outside. I shivered,and thought gloomily of swaying portieres, creaking doors, and banging shutters. I hated the house at any time, but in a high wind it seemed to become a place of horror.

I forced myself to get up, and I hastily tidied my appearance. I went out into the hall and found that no one had turned on the light, and it was almost totally dark. I took a step toward the light switch—and stopped short, with a sick feeling at the pit of my stomach.

The old man was dragging himself across the attic floor again.

CHAPTER
11

I STOOD QUITE STILL in the gloom, dimly conscious that I was very cold and that I was trembling. I was trying to gather sufficient courage to get to the light switch when I was enveloped in a fresh wave of terror. There was a figure, standing dark and still, at the other end of the hall.

I remember putting my hand over my mouth and trying to whisper something, and suddenly the silence was broken with scream after shrill scream, which echoed and reechoed through the house. I gasped and flew across to the light switch and had to claw desperately for a moment before I could get it on.

I looked then and saw that it was Freda. It was impossible to tell whether the dragging was still going on, for her shrieks drowned out every other sound. By the time I got down to her, she had a ring of people around her, all trying to quiet her at once.

She stopped screaming—I think she must certainly have been too exhausted to go on—and began to babble hysterically.

"It means another Ballinger. One of us must go—it's either Berg or me. Aunt Mabel and Rhynda don't count—they haven't any Ballinger blood. You'd better say your prayers, Berg, it's you or me.

Only it doesn't matter, because we're all going to be wiped out, all the Ballingers."

Several people spoke to her and tried to soothe her, and I glanced over my shoulder and noticed that Joe was on the fringe of the group. He was leaning against the wall and chewing on a toothpick. I nudged Berg, and he looked around.

"What's all the excitement?" Joe asked lazily.

I don't know whether Freda heard him or not, but she began to talk wildly about the dragging noise, and he interested himself sufficiently to question her. It took him five minutes to extract a fairly coherent recital of what she had heard, and when he had got it at last, he departed immediately to investigate the attic.

I was calm enough by then to notice that Rhynda and Richard were in the group and to feel a sense of satisfaction about it. I had thought that they might stay out for dinner, and I was definitely annoyed that Rhynda, who should be in mourning, would calmly appropriate the only date and outing that I had had for many months. I was chewing it over in my mind when Berg took me firmly by the arm and led me to the stairs.

"Come on down, Leigh, I want to talk to you," he said quietly.

We descended to one of the small rooms, of which there were no less than four, that opened off the main hall. This particular one was a sort of music room, I suppose, for it had an ancient upright piano in one corner and an empty music rack in another. I sat down and looked at Berg inquiringly, but he shook his head and explained briefly, "I'm waiting for Dick."

Richard appeared after a short delay.

"I thought I was lost," he said. "I've wandered through three other rooms exactly like this one looking for you, and I didn't think I'd ever get back to civilization again. You could be lost for weeks in this museum—you ought to provide guests with a permanent equipment of hardtack and water, just in case."

Berg said nervously, "Shut up, Dick. What's that fellow Joe doing?"

"He has a chair up in the attic, and he says he's going to sit there and wait until the noise starts up again."

"It may be days," I murmured thoughtfully. "In fact, I hope it is."

Berg gave me a crooked smile. "Association with a bunch of loopy Ballingers is spoiling your disposition."

"Leigh," said Richard suddenly, "did you ever hear that noise before we came?"

"Just once," I said slowly, and told them of the time Mrs. Ballinger and I had heard it. I told them, too, about the footsteps that had gone down the stairs and out the front door.

That interested them, as I knew it would, and in the end I broke my promise to Freda and told them her story of having seen who had moved John. They got quite excited about that, but I was firm about making them promise not to mention it to her.

"If we can get together on all this," Berg said, rumpling his hair, "Joe has a couple of deputies, and I think they intend to keep an eye on things, but I'm uneasy. I suggest we snoop around a bit and if we haven't uncovered anything by tomorrow night, I believe we should send for a private detective. I know you two haven't anything to do with all this, but I—well, I ask you as my friends, to help me."

Richard and I agreed at once to do anything that we could, and Berg turned to me.

"Then I'd like you to get after Freda and see of you can force her to tell who it was she saw moving John."

Richard opened the lid of the piano and stared absently at the dusty, discolored keys. "I shouldn't bank too strongly on that angle, Berg," he said, without looking up. "Remember, her accusation of Amy was pretty twisted."

"I know—but it was true up to a point. She *had* seen Amy cutting a rope." He reflected for a moment and turned to me again. "Another thing, Leigh. Try and find out what Amy and Freda are at each other's throats about."

I nodded, and we both looked at Richard, who was picking out "America" with one finger on the piano.

"Dick!" Berg said sharply.

"Hmm?"

"I'd like you to follow Joe and his henchmen around and keep abreast of anything new that they may pick up. I'm going to study that noise in the attic. If I have to sit up all night and every night I'm going to get to the bottom of it."

Richard closed the piano. "You have one thing to start on there," he suggested. Berg and I stared at him, and he went on slowly, "The two times we heard that noise the wind has been blowing a gale and howling around the house. There may be some connection."

Berg considered it, and I said eagerly, "I remember, now, that the night Mrs. Ballinger and I heard it, before you all came, there was a high wind blowing."

"Perhaps there is some connection," Berg admitted, and he left the room rather suddenly with a purposeful look on his face. I started to rise from the small settee where I had been curled up, but Richard came and lowered himself into it and pulled me back beside him.

"One moment," he said. "I have a bone to pick with you."

"I didn't know there was that much food in the house," I said brightly.

He rather absently possessed himself of my hand, and spreading it out on his own, regarded it thoughtfully.

"No amount of wit and airy persiflage is going to save you from facing the issue. I want to know—in fact, I damn well demand to know—why you brought Rhynda along on our date this afternoon. Could you have been feeling the need of a chaperon?"

"You flatter yourself," I said bitterly. "I didn't want Rhynda along at all. But she asked me point-blank where you were, and when I explained, she said she'd go too. She even beat me to the front seat."

He chuckled and closed his hand up, with mine inside it.

"You talk too much, Smithy. Explanations and alibis are feeble stuff, and people are apt to judge by results. Had you been smart enough, you could have saved the occasion somehow."

"The occasion really wasn't worth struggling for," I said, trying to draw my hand away.

But he tightened his hold and murmured, "Thanks, Smithy, thanks. And now for a few girlish confidences. I aim to get married some time this year."

I felt suddenly cold and remote. I stared at the opposite wall and said flippantly, "You'll have to hurry it up, then. You've only a few days left."

"You're so literal," he sighed. "Next year, then."

"What is she like?" I asked, trying to be casual.

"I really couldn't say."

I turned and looked at him. "You don't know what she's like, and yet you've made up your mind to marry her? In that case, she must be rich."

"A dirty crack," he decided, after a moment's thought, "and quite uncalled for." He turned his hand over, and mine with it, and seemed to be studying my fingernails. "To clear up a possible misunderstanding, I have not yet decided on my future bride."

I relaxed against the back of the settee and said piously, "Then there's hope for all of us. Incidentally, what's your hurry?"

His eyes wandered to my hair and he stretched a lazy arm and wound a strand around his finger. "It's my mother, you know. She'd like to see me safely married. She's afraid I'll be an old maid if it goes on much longer."

I nodded sympathetically, and he went on, laughing a little. "Will you come and visit my family sometime, Smithy, to see if they approve, in case I decide on you?"

"No," I said primly. "If you decide on me, they'll have to take me blind."

"That's hardly fair, Smithy."

Before I could reply, Mrs. Ballinger burst into the room like a whirlwind.

"Leigh!" she shrieked. "What do you mean by sitting here calmly, when Freda has completely disappeared?"

CHAPTER
12

WE BOTH SPRANG UP and I felt the weight of the house drop heavily over me again.

"How long have you missed her?" Richard asked

"I don't know," she wailed, wringing her hands. "Berg just told me. He's looked everywhere."

We went out into the hall, Mrs. Ballinger talking excitedly all the time. I managed to gather from her that Rhynda and Berg were both searching, that dinner was ready, and that Amy and Donald were drinking firewater of some sort in the living room. Mrs. Ballinger and Richard disappeared towards the rear of the house, and I went directly to the living room, where Amy and her boy friend were sitting cozily over their cocktails.

Amy gave me a dirty look, but Donald Tait rose and asked courteously, "May I pour you one, Miss Smith?"

Amy and I spoke together. I said, "Thanks," and Amy said there was enough only for two, and it was their own liquor.

Donald murmured, "Don't be crude, darling," and I finished the drink in one gulp. I had a hazy idea that if Freda were in the house at all she would be somewhere close to Donald and Amy, and I began to move slowly around the shadowy room, looking to see if she were curled up in any of the large chairs.

"What are you doing now?" Amy asked irritably, obviously anxious to hound me out of the room.

"Looking for Freda," I said amiably and peered behind the heavy drapes at one of the windows.

Donald looked up quickly and asked, "What's happened to Freda?"

"Disappeared," I said briefly.

Amy was pouring the last drops of the cocktail mixture into her glass. "You're crazy to bother," she said. "You know Freda—she's hiding out just to annoy us."

Donald looked full at her. "You should have told me. Whether she's hiding on purpose or not, she must be found. You shouldn't be so obvious in your method, Amy."

He left the room, and I was aching to see Amy's face, but I had my back to her, and I did not want to be obvious in my method either. I think she finished her drink first, and then I heard her flounce out after him. She never left him alone for very long.

Most of the rooms in the house had large closets, and the living room had a super closet. It was cluttered with odds and ends and coated over with dust, and I had long suspected it of housing a thriving colony of mice. I had left it until the last because of the mice, but it was there I found Freda. I thought she looked a bit wild-eyed, and she would not come out until I had assured her that there was no one around.

"What were you doing in there?" I asked curiously.

She brushed ineffectively at the dust in her clothes and blinked owlishly in the light. "I heard them make a date for cocktails before dinner, just the two of them, so I planted myself in the closet to hear what they had to say. I would have heard something, too, only you had to come in and spoil things."

"Something about John's death?" I said quickly.

"John's death?" she repeated vaguely. "Oh, yes. Of course."

She was obviously lying, but before I could pump her further, Mrs. Ballinger burst into the room and fell on her neck. Freda dis-

entangled herself, and in answer to her aunt's questions and re-
proaches denied that she had been missing, refused an explanation,
and gave it as her opinion that it was a pity a person could not be
alone for a while without the whole household making a fuss. Mrs.
Ballinger had to let it go at that and presently went off to send the
word about that Freda had been found, and we were all to go in to
dinner.

Dinner was more strained and unpleasant than usual that night,
because Joe was with us. I don't know what right he had to be there,
if any, and I think Mrs. Ballinger was on the verge of ordering him
out. But I believe she was a little in awe of Joe, in spite of herself, and
after directing a couple of long black looks at him, she left him in
peace and turned her attention to other matters.

She entered into a minor skirmish with Amy and was finally vic-
torious in making Amy sit nearly the table length away from Donald
Tait. She directed me to go and get a sofa pillow, and when I returned with it, she insisted on stuffing it behind Rhynda. Rhynda
protested to no purpose and was forced to finish her meal sitting on
a bias, but Mrs Ballinger beamed at her and seemed to feel that her
delicate condition had been suitably provided for.

We were all rather silent, which was a mistake, because when Joe
was eating one heard the whole process quite clearly. I was considering excusing myself when Joe pushed his plate away, produced a
toothpick, and announced that he'd heard Miss Ballinger had disappeared and been found again. He wanted to know where she'd been,
and why.

Freda refused to answer, and Mrs. Ballinger said quickly, "It was
all a mistake. We thought she had disappeared, but she had not."

Berg and Rosalie Hannahs supported this statement in chorus,
and Joe looked us all over with an expression that assured us he was
on to the fact that we were merely trying to avoid further questioning. But he grunted and let the matter rest.

We sat around in the living room after dinner and gave an involuntary but very good imitation of people in a dentist's waiting room.
I asked Freda to come up to my bedroom for a chat, but she gave me
a sidelong look and refused.

Mrs. Ballinger talked about the funeral that was to be held in the
morning, but no one seemed to be listening. At about nine o'clock
Richard and Berg went out, and I supposed that they were getting on

with the investigation business. Rhynda left soon afterwards, and I felt sure she had gone after Richard and found myself sniffing.

I changed the direction of my thoughts and determined to get after Freda and make her talk. She was sitting in a straight chair,with her hands folded, staring at nothing. I edged over to her and said softly, "Wouldn't you like to sleep with me tonight, Freda?"

She looked up quickly and said almost breathlessly, "Yes, I would. It's kind of you."

"Then let's go up now. Tomorrow won't be easy, and we'd better get as much sleep as we can."

She assented listlessly, and we said good night to the others. Mrs. Hannahs was busy with some complicated knitting, Mrs. Ballinger was still droning on about the funeral, and Amy had picked up a magazine and was bent over it, studying it closely. Donald Tait sat apart, staring at the window and smoking innumerable cigarettes.

As we went upstairs, I thought with regret of my comfortable double bed. I hated having to share it with Freda, but I felt that it was all in the line of duty. I was confident that I could get her to talk, sooner or later.

As we undressed, I started to pump her, but it was like hitting against a stone wall. She sidestepped me every time, and at last she began to talk about a red sweater that she planned to knit for herself when and if she got back to town. She seemed to think that with the red sweater to set her off, she would look so attractive that certain troubles she had had would be smoothed away.

"What kind of trouble?" I asked.

"Oh well, not real trouble. But I haven't been looking as well as I might, and I intend to do something about it."

I was diverted, in spite of myself, and started to tell her delicately just how to improve her dressing and her general appearance. She brushed me and my ideas aside impatiently. "You don't understand my type," she said with finality.

I gave it up and let her prattle on. She seemed to have cheered up considerably, and I supposed it was because she did not have to face sleeping alone.

From time to time I heard sounds of the others coming up and going to their rooms, and after a while the house settled into silence. The wind dropped, and I glanced behind the drawn shade at the window and saw that there was a bright moon. Freda said suddenly,

"I'm tired. Let's put out the light and go to sleep. We'll go to the bathroom first, though. If we go together it won't be so scary."

I agreed, and we went out and down the hall, but when we got to the bathroom door, she came over modest and said, "You wait here until I come out—or would you rather go in first?"

"Go ahead," I said resignedly, and she slipped in. I heard her lock the door and reflected, with faint amusement, that she probably would not use a bathroom that could not be properly locked. I heard her turn on the basin faucet, and I scuffed around impatiently and hoped that she would not take the time to brush her teeth.

There was no sound from any of the rooms, and the house was oppressively quiet. I thought of the noise in the attic and shivered nervously. I was about to call through the door and tell Freda to hurry when I heard a faucet jerked on, and water running into the bathtub.

I was instantly furious. She had no right to expect me to kick around in the hall while she took a bath! I marched back to my room indignantly, flung myself on the bed, and lit a cigarette.

I was far from relaxed, however. I kept glancing uneasily at the door, half-afraid that something or somebody would come creeping through. The dead silence seemed to press heavily on my ears, and at last I crushed out my cigarette and got up from the bed, because I had to do something.

I went out into the hall again and walked quickly down to the bathroom. I listened at the door, but there was no sound of any kind. I was conscious of my quickened breathing, and my hands were clammy. There should be some sort of movement! My fears started to rush up in a panic, and I had to stand still for a moment and whisper fiercely, "Don't be a fool! Don't be a fool!"

I took a long breath, tapped on the door, and called softly, "Freda."

There was no answer and no sound. I had been vaguely conscious that the light was still on in the bathroom, because I could see the glow at the end of the door. It dawned on me now, rather suddenly, that the door could no longer be locked, or even properly closed, since I knew that it fitted well and had no cracks.

Then Freda had probably left, perhaps gone to her room for something she had forgotten.

I put my hand on the door and gave it a tentative push, and it swung back far enough to reveal a chair. Freda's nightgown and dressing gown had been thrown over its back. I gripped the door-knob and felt panic stir in me again. She was still here, then—still in her bath—and when she had locked the door, it had not caught properly. I pushed the door wide and stepped into the room.

The bathtub was half-filled with water, and Freda lay in it, face down.

CHAPTER
13

I STOOD GAPING FOOLISHLY at the still body and thinking helplessly that Freda would hate to have me see her in the nude.

As sense came back to me, I felt a scream coming on, but I managed to bottle it. I wheeled about, fled into the hall, and banged wildly on several of the closed doors. I leaned against the wall for a moment, panting, and was thrown into action again by the sudden thought that Freda might still be alive. It had not been so long—
I raced back to the bathroom and began to tug frantically at Freda's shoulders, but I could not raise her. I shuddered and let her go, and at the same minute, I thought of the drain. I opened it and realized bitterly that it was the first thing I should have done.

Several people crowded into the bathroom then, and I gladly faded into the background. Richard and Donald Tait lifted her out of the bathtub and laid her on the floor. They tried resuscitation of some sort, but I did not stay to watch.

I hurried downstairs to telephone for the doctor. On the way down, and while I gave the number to the operator, I thought only of what I had to do, but while I waited for my connection I glanced around at all the dark empty rooms that yawned away from the hall and was suddenly hanging on desperately to what little control I had left.

Dr. O'Beirne promised to come at once, and I hung up, opened the front door and left it ajar, and flew up the stairs, all well within a minute.

They had carried Freda to her bedroom, and Rhynda told me they had found a nasty wound on her head. Rhynda looked near to collapse. She told me, not once but several times, that Freda must have slipped while she was getting into the bath.

I agreed with her at last. "Of course that's what happened," I said soothingly. "She slipped and hit her head and fainted."

Rhynda sighed and seemed to relax a little, and I put an arm around her and urged her towards her bedroom. She came quietly enough, and I helped her into bed and gave her one of Mrs. Ballinger's sleeping tablets. I went straight back to the bathroom, where I found Richard on his hands and knees beside the bathtub.

"What are you looking for?" I asked.

He raised his head and said in a preoccupied voice, "I was looking for some marks of where she hit her head when she slipped."

"Don't waste your time," I said and was duly surprised to hear that my voice was unnaturally high and loud. "If you want to get anywhere with your little magnifying glass and cloth cap act, then you'd better look for a weapon." Unexpectedly, even to myself, I followed this statement with a shrill giggle.

He got to his feet and pushed me firmly down onto the chair. "Take it easy, Smithy, and tell me what you mean."

I twisted my hands together, swallowed twice, and said almost steadily, "In the first place, Freda locked the door when she went in. I was standing close to it, and on thinking back, I realize that there can be no mistake about it. Then she turned on the basin tap, and shortly afterward, the bath tap.

"Freda would never unlock the door if she were going to take a bath, so I feel certain that somebody was already in here, waiting for her. And you'd better look for a weapon."

He nodded slowly. "It sounds right enough, but how could whoever was waiting for Freda know that she would come in first? It might have been any one of the others."

"It wouldn't matter," I declared, and indicated the unusual size of the room with a wave of my arm. "There are no less than three closets big enough to hold a person who wanted to hide. One of them even locks on the inside."

"Which one?" he said quickly.

I showed him the closet that had been built in originally, presumably to hold the linen supply. The other two were merely the two sides of a large armoire. The linen closet had a key on the inside of the door, and I remembered Mrs. Ballinger telling me that it had been on the inside since some long-forgotten Ballinger child had playfully locked a housemaid in and left her to pound wildly on the door an entire morning.

Richard opened it and we peered in. It was quite bare and very dusty. I had made it a firm rule never to dust closets.

Richard stooped down and examined the floor carefully. "This is the place, all right," he said soberly. "It's all scuffed about."

"What's all scuffed about?" I asked anxiously.

"The dust. I know your housekeeping methods, Smithy, and this floor should present a smooth surface of dust, with occasional curlicues of fluff. The dust is here, but it's been disturbed."

"Aren't there any footprints?"

He straightened and looked down at me patronizingly. "There should be, of course, two perfect specimens that I could match up with somebody's shoes. And then I could hand the owner of the shoes over to Joe."

"I didn't expect anything like that," I said. "But isn't there half a print? Some sort of outline?"

He smiled at me annoyingly and shook his head. "There's not even a quarter of an eighth. And even supposing there were? Hasn't it occurred to you that it might easily have been made by someone who came here on a perfectly innocent errand?"

"Who would be coming to an empty unused closet on an innocent errand?" I ask huffily..

"How about Mrs. Ballinger, to check up on your housekeeping? But have a look for yourself."

I knelt down and saw at once that he was right. The dust had been disturbed, but the floor was bare of anything except a plain pin. I picked it up and absentmindedly stuck it in the collar of my dressing gown. As I straightened up, I heard Joe's voice behind us.

"What are youse doing here?" it asked ominously.

I turned around. "Has Dr. O'Beirne come?"

"Yeah, with me. Did you know the front door was open?"

"I opened it," I said shortly.

"Oh. Well, what are you doing here?"

"We're giving a kaffeeklatsch," I said and received a violent nudge in the back from Richard.

"What?" said Joe puzzled.

I glanced at Richard, who stared back at me without expression.

"We were looking for a mark where Miss Ballinger bumped her head when she slipped," I explained glibly, with some idea that it would be better to let Joe find out the worst by himself.

"So she slipped," Joe observed and spread it thickly with sarcasm.

"We don't know," I admitted.

"But you'd just as soon put the idea around?"

Richard took over for me. "We're not suggesting anything. We
don't know what happened, but we naturally assumed that she had
slipped. Of course, all that's up to you."

He took my arm and started to urge me from the room, but Joe
planted himself squarely in our way.

"Now just a minute. I want to hear what you know about this."

Richard did not know anything and said so. He had been in his
room all the time, and had come out when I banged on his door. I
told my story, and of course Joe put me through it properly. By the
time I had finished, his eyes were narrowed to slits, and he was looking at me as if he had got his man.

"You heard her lock the door," he said slowly, "and then you
come back and find it open, and still, you wanta make out she slipped."

"Perhaps, when she turned the lock, it did not catch," I suggested,
a bit feebly.

Joe promptly turned and examined the lock, moving it backwards and forwards, and at last straightened up triumphantly. He
put on the velvet glove and inquired gently, "You say you have been
living here since the spring?"

I admitted it, warily.

"Then you should know that this lock doesn't make any noise at
all, unless it catches. So, if you heard Miss Ballinger lock it, it was
locked."

"All right," I said wearily. "It was locked. Now let me out of here."

Joe moved aside but called after me almost immediately, "Another thing. You shouldn't have touched the body or anything before
I got here."

I turned around and gave him a chilly stare. "It was just that we
thought the body might still be alive. Of course, next time, since you
wish it, we won't consider that angle."

I marched on again but my head was swimming. "Next time—
next time," I thought wildly. "My God! Surely there won't be any
more. What on earth made me say that?"

I glanced back and saw that Richard had remained in the bathroom, and remembered that he was supposed to keep abreast of

Joe's discoveries. I thought miserably that I had failed completely on my part of the job, and I wondered how far Berg had got with his.

I went to Freda's bedroom and found that Dr. O'Beirne had finished and had covered her with a sheet. Mrs. Ballinger stood on one side of the bed, having a mild attack of hysterics, while Berg patted her shoulder and murmured to her.

Amy stood on the other side, staring down at the sheeted figure and silently wringing her hands. Donald Tait was just inside the door, leaning against the wall and apparently staring at his feet. Rosalie Hannahs was crying quietly in a rocking chair.

Dr. O'Beirne was just leaving the room and spoke to me at the door. "We're going to do an autopsy. I'll come back at about seven with the ambulance."

I glanced at his wristwatch and saw that it was half past two. I nodded to him, and he went off down the hall and into the bathroom. He spoke to Joe, and I heard Joe say, "No, I'm staying here." He came out then and went downstairs, and I followed him and closed the front door after him when he left.

I hurried upstairs again and saw Richard and Joe emerge from the bathroom. They were not actually arm in arm, but they gave the same impression of chumminess, and they were talking amiably together. They approached me without any sign of recognition, but after they had passed Richard looked over his shoulder, winked at me, and said out of the corner of his mouth, "Coffee."

They went down the stairs, and I went on to Freda's room. It was empty except for Rosalie Hannahs, and she stood just inside the door, looking decidedly uncomfortable. She welcomed me with a little gasp of relief.

"Oh, Miss Smith! Won't you stay here for a while? I feel terribly inadequate, but I simply can't stand it any longer. Mrs. Ballinger insisted that someone must stay with her, and Miss Perrin has gone to bed. She said she'd be back, but I know she won't. Mrs. Ballinger won't allow Mr. Tait to stay here because he's married, and Berg is up in the attic and declares he will not rest until he gets to the bottom of it all."

I eased her into the hall and said firmly, "Get to bed and get as much sleep as you can. I'll take care of all this."

She smiled at me gratefully and hurried away, and I closed Freda's door and locked it from the outside. Then I went around to my room and locked the connecting door. On my way down the hall, I wondered a little anxiously whether there was enough coffee for a pot now and another pot at breakfast. I knew that all the supplies were very low, and Mrs. Ballinger, despite her troubles, was still tightly gripping the purse strings. If she found out that we were wasting coffee by drinking it at three o'clock in the morning, she was quite capable of recommending a glass of hot water as a healthful breakfast beverage.

As I passed Rhynda's door, I was diverted by the sound of her voice, and I slowed up to listen. I could not make anything of it and because I was a little uneasy about her, I opened the door a crack and peered in.

She was talking in her sleep in an odd, high whine, and it was unintelligible until she suddenly said quite clearly, "The baby must die."

CHAPTER
14

I BACKED OUT HASTILY and closed the door. I was shivering, and I tightened my bathrobe and told myself firmly that Rhynda was undoubtedly under a terrific strain, and that if she were really pregnant, her situation was very unfortunate. I made up my mind to try and get in touch with her relatives so that they could take her away and look after her. I went down to the kitchen and found Joe and Richard seated at the table, busily eating. There was a third place laid.

"For whom?" I asked, airing my grammar.

"Youse," said Richard.

I sat down and poured myself some coffee. "How did you know I was coming?"

He piled some food onto my plate and said kindly, "You always do. I never saw such a nose for refreshments in all my life."

"If you'd lived in this place for nearly nine months, you'd be constantly hungry, too," I said aggrievedly.

"I am constantly hungry, anyway. But, at that, I think Joe is the greatest trencherman of us all."

"No," said Joe, with his mouth full, "I never even got overseas. Still in trainin' camp when the armistice came."

Richard and I stopped chewing to stare at him, but he had his face in his plate again and took no further notice of us. It dawned on me, with sudden horror, that we were eating herring again.

"Richard!" I said weakly. "This fish—we ate it last night."

"That was another one. Do you ever tell lies, Smithy? You declared there's be a row about that first herring, and nothing happened."

"Because she decided to save it for Sunday. But there will be a row, now that we've eaten it twice."

"You'd better know the facts," he said firmly. "This afternoon, while you presumably were napping, Amy, Rosalie, Donald and I somehow became entangled in a game of bridge, and we were in the midst of the first scrap when Doris walked in on us. She said that what with Joe the well-known hog around—"

"The food here's terrible," Joe interposed idly.

"It seemed," Richard continued, "that there was not so much as a piece of moldy cheese left in the house."

"She puts it in the mousetraps if it gets moldy," I murmured.

"Doris gave us a list of groceries, explained that she did not want to bother Mrs. Ballinger, and asked us if we would see to it. She said we were to charge the things, as Mrs. Ballinger had an account at the store. We piled into my car, went to the village, and bought all the things on the list."

"Even so," I said after a moment, "this herring was not meant for us."

"On the contrary," said Richard, "I bought it expressly for us. Mrs. Ballinger may have one of the others."

"One of the others?" I repeated hollowly.

"Smithy," he said patiently, "won't you realize that you have been fired, and that Mrs. Ballinger will have to kick somebody else's teeth in when she gets the bill?"

"She's forgotten about it," I said wearily, "and, unfortunately, I'll have to forget it, too, until I save a bit more money. Now please tell me how many herrings you bought, and what else."

He considered for a moment and then laughed reminiscently. "My only extravagance was the herrings. I bought six of them." I gasped, and he explained, "I noticed you liked them, and I thought it was a cheap way of keeping Joe stuffed."

"Beefsteak is more in my line," Joe said ungratefully.

"The rest of the order was entirely Amy's affair," Richard continued, "and it would be easier to tell you what she didn't buy than otherwise. When she finally worked her way around to the liquor counter, I did point out that her aunt Mabel was a teetotaler, but she ignored me. She bought everything for a cocktail bar except the chairs and tables. The grocer had tears in his eyes when we left."

I clutched at my head and moaned. "Mrs. Ballinger will have a stroke when she gets that bill, after all that's happened to her—"

"Is she broke?" Joe asked.

"No," I said, "but she just doesn't like to spend money."

Joe nodded tolerantly. "I'm that way myself. I started out with nothing, and today I can sign my name to a check for ten thousand or better." He tilted his chair back, produced his toothpick, and surveyed us triumphantly.

"Nice work," said Richard admiringly. "Don't forget to send us a check when we get married."

Joe let his chair down with a bang and leaned forward, narrowing his eyes. "Are youse two planning to get married?"

Richard nodded sunnily. "Not necessarily to each other, of course, but in that case, you can split the check in half."

Joe relaxed and said, "Oh. Wise guy, eh?"

"Conceited, too," I supplied. "I don't care for his beauty myself. I prefer your type. More virile, you know."

Joe ran a reflective hand over what was left of his hair, then jammed it suddenly into his pocket and shot me a suspicious look.

"That won't get you nowhere, lady."

I said, "Oh," and gave him one of Amy's best pouts.

"How could I become a virile type, Joe?" Richard asked.

"If it means what I think it means," Joe said disapprovingly, "she oughta be ashamed of herself talkin' about such things in front of two guys she don't hardly know. Now let's get down to business. I want to know the financial status of this family."

"Do you understand what he means by financial status, Smithy?" Richard asked kindly. "Or shall I explain it to you?"

"You keep outa this, Jones," said the Law. "Now I tried to question the old lady about it, but she shut up like a clam and acted like I was tryin' to sell her a gold mine. I'm gettin' in touch with her lawyer, so I'll find out about it anyways. But maybe you can give me a rough idea so I can get on with it."

I told him what I knew of the trust fund for John, Berg and Freda but admitted that I could only guess at the state of Mrs. Ballinger's finances. I believed, though, that her money had been put into insurance annuities for herself, which meant that when she died she would leave nothing but the house.

"And who gets the house, in that case?" Joe asked.

But I did not know. I felt convinced that she had not made a will, for I knew that she hated any mention or thought of her death, and I did not think that she had planned for it in any way.

Joe dropped it and returned to the trust fund. "Now that these two Ballingers are dead, does the third one get their share as well as his own?"

I didn't know that either. Richard said thoughtfully, "Probably Berg does get it. I don't know whether there was any provision for Rhynda in connection with it, but I think not."

"What about the baby?" Joe asked bluntly.

Richard shook his head. "Nothing to do with the trust fund, I'm pretty sure. But I know John has left Rhynda well provided for quite apart from that."

I raised my hand suddenly at that point to brush the hair away from my face and scratched myself badly on the pin that I had stuck into the collar of my bathrobe. I pulled it out impatiently and looked at it for a moment before I remembered that I had picked it up from the floor of the closet in the bathroom.

I noticed that it differed from an ordinary pin in that it had a black head, although that was the only difference. I said nothing about it but put it back into my collar and privately decided to search the house in the morning and find out if there were any more like it.

Joe yawned loudly, stretched, let his chair down with a bang, and got to his feet. "I'm gonna sleep it off till the boys come," he announced. "Guess I'll have this thing cleared up by tomorrow night."

We followed him out of the kitchen and watched him settle down on a couch in the living room. He seemed to go to sleep on the way down, because he was no sooner settled than he gave a gentle snore.

"Quite a talent, that," said Richard admiringly. He turned to me and added severely, "Come on. It's time you were in bed. You keep the most abominable hours!"

We went up the stairs, and I said tiredly, "It's all been so horrible! I don't feel as though I'd ever sleep straight through the night again." He took my hand and squeezed it, and we walked down the hall to my door.

"Breakfast at nine," I said, "and the funeral's at eleven."

He nodded. He was looking down at me and did not seem to be thinking of either breakfast or the funeral. "Get a good night's sleep, Smithy, and try to put the whole thing out of your mind." He leaned toward me without haste and kissed me on the lips. "Just a sample, and I hope it shows Bill up as a tyro and a mug."

He went off towards his own room, and I backed rather hastily into mine. The reading lamp over the bed was lighted as I had left it, and I did not turn on the main switch. I locked the door, threw my dressing gown over a chair, and got into bed quickly. I turned off the light, drew the bedclothes up to my chin, and sighed with relief as I felt my body relaxing. The moon was very bright, and after my eyes had become accustomed to the darkness, I could see the larger objects in the room fairly well. I could see the rocking chair at the foot of the bed.

Suddenly, with a shuddering gasp and a violent jerking of all my muscles, I was sitting erect.

Freda was in the rocking chair, her face turned to the window and shining with a greenish pallor in the moonlight.

CHAPTER
15

I HAVE NO RECOLLECTION of it, but I must have put on the reading light, for they found it on later. I got to the door,somehow and struggled madly with the lock, but my fingers were numb and I could not seem to make them work properly. The door gave suddenly at last, and I stumbled out into the hall. My legs gave way then, and I fell onto the carpet. I could not get up again, but I cried out and was hazily conscious of a door opening down the hall.

I was not clearly aware of anything more until I found myself in Rhynda's room, with Rhynda and Rosalie Hannahs shaking their heads over me. I looked at them dully and started to tell them that I was cold, and then I remembered about Freda sitting in the rocking chair with her mouth stretched in a stiff grin and her eyes staring sightlessly into the moonlight, and I began to shiver violently, with my teeth chattering.

Rosalie pulled the bedclothes up around my neck and talked to me in a low voice. She told me that I must be quiet, and that I would not have to sleep alone again, that Rhynda wanted me to share her room.

"She has the twin beds there, and she's nervous herself, so we'll just move all your things in."

I glanced at Rhynda, who nodded and said that she had suggested the arrangement because she could not stand being alone any more. I felt myself relaxing a bit, and Rosalie presently brought me one of Mrs. Ballinger's sleeping tablets and a glass of water.

I swallowed the tablet and thought vaguely that they must be running low, we had used so many of them since John's death. I could see Mrs. Ballinger telling Joe that he must clear up the mystery because she could not stand the sleeping-tablet upkeep, and I had to struggle to keep from shrieking with laughter at the idea. I went to sleep after a while.

Doris woke me at half past nine the next morning. She told me I'd have to get started if I wanted to make the funeral, and when I rolled over, I was astonished to see that she had my breakfast on a tray. The other bed was empty, and Rhynda's dressing gown lying over a chair and a drifting of powder along the mirror indicated that she had dressed and gone down.

I thanked Doris profusely for the breakfast, since I knew that breakfast in bed was against her principles. She settled another pillow behind my back and told me that they had taken Freda away and that her funeral was to be on Tuesday.

"But are they sure—I mean, was she really dead?"

"Dead as a herring," said Doris firmly. "I don't guess they know, though, whether she drowned or was killed when she was hit over the head."

I shuddered. "I feel as though it were my fault somehow. I was right there with her. I shouldn't have let her go into the bathroom alone."

"Don't you worry about it, dearie," she said kindly. "It's silly to blame yourself for anything, just as though you could help it!"

She went off, and I ate my breakfast and dressed quickly. I cleaned up the bathroom and tidied Rhynda's room and made the beds, and then I swore to myself that that was all the housework I intended to do. I went out to the hall and ran directly into Joe. He was furious.

"Can't leave a damn thing alone for a minute around here without somebody meddling." He stared hard at me. "Do you know who's been foolin' in the bathroom?"

I'm sure I went pale. "Er—foolin'?" I said weakly.

"Who cleaned up in there?"

"Well, it—it was messy," I stammered. "I did clean up a bit. I always do, every day."

He gave me a long cold stare and turned on his heel. "You've washed all my clues away," he said bitterly and loped off down the hall.

I stood looking after him and feeling a bit troubled. I supposed that I should not have touched the bathroom, but then, I thought irritably, why doesn't he lock the door so that no one can spoil his clues? And remembered immediately that he could hardly lock us all out of the only bathroom in the house.

Brief funeral services for John were held in the village undertaking parlors. It was very cold, and the whole thing was inexpressibly dreary. Rhynda and Rosalie Hannahs cried quietly throughout the service, and Mrs. Ballinger blew her nose vigorously several times. Berg stared at the floor without expression.

Amy misbehaved herself, as usual. She kept tapping her foot audibly and looking impatiently around the room. It was very obvious that she wanted to be done with the whole thing. I saw Donald Tait nudge her twice when she became too noisy and restless.

They buried John in the old Ballinger plot in the bleak little cemetery, and then we all headed for home. Doris had a very tasty lunch waiting for us, and the food was so plentiful that Mrs. Ballinger emerged from her grief and eyed it suspiciously. However, she made no comment, and we presently went to the living room where some of us smoked while the others talked of the funeral in low voices.

I noticed that the room was in a mess. Newspapers were strewn about, ashtrays filled to overflowing, and there was dust over everything.

Mrs. Ballinger looked it over and then called to me imperiously. "Leigh! Why haven't you seen to this room?"

"It's no concern of mine," I said coldly. "You discharged me."

She frowned and tapped on the arm of her chair with impatient fingers. "You'd better consider yourself employed again. I can't have this mess around."

"Then I must ask for five dollars a week increase and not so much work." I was conscious of the fact that Richard was grinning at me, but I kept my eyes carefully away from him.

Mrs. Ballinger continued to beat agitatedly on the arm of her chair, and her face grew red. "I cannot pay you any more," she said at last. "Your salary is ample, and there are plenty of girls who would jump at the job."

"Then you had better get in touch with one of them. Perhaps Amy can help you out until you make some arrangement."

Amy jerked her head out of her magazine and said promptly, "Not me. I don't know the first thing about housework. You'll have to pick on someone else."

"You don't have to know anything about it, Amy," I said kindly. "It will come to you as you go along, and if you need advice, don't hesitate to come to me."

I left the room, and after a brief hesitation in the hall, decided that this would be as good a time as any to go upstairs and search for the black-headed pins. I started in Mrs. Ballinger's room after making up my mind to play no favorites. I intended to search even my own room. It did not take me five minutes to realize that somebody else was going through the bedrooms thoroughly, too. I nearly ran into him, once or twice, and at last I got a glimpse of him. It was Joe.

I took care to keep out of his sight after that, but I knew he was getting uneasy. Once he called out, "Who's there?" and I crouched down behind a chair and did not answer. I knew the house so well that it was easy for me to avoid running into him.

We continued with our search, and after a while I began to feel the need for a notebook and pencil. I wanted to write down some of the curious things I found in the various rooms so that I would not forget them.

Providentially, I came across a small leather-bound shopping list with an attached pencil on Rosalie's bureau. It did not seem to have been used, so I borrowed it and jotted down the things I had discovered and in which rooms.

When I had only Freda's room and my own left to search, I heard Joe give voice to what must have been an explosion of nerves. He swore loudly and freely and bellowed out that whoever was following him had better stop it and come out into the open.

I was in Freda's room when this crisis developed, so I slipped through the connecting door to my own room, kicked my shoes off, stretched out on the bed, and pretended to be asleep. I had barely arranged myself when Joe burst in. He stopped short, breathed heavily for a moment, and said, "Very pretty—you're doin' fine."

I stirred drowsily and opened one eye.

"You can save those antics for Jones," said Joe rudely. "You ain't foolin' me. It just so happens that this was the room I was searchin' before I went to the hall to find out who was tailin' me. So there hasn't been time for you to go to bed and get to sleep."

"Embarrassing," I admitted and sat up. "In that case, I'll talk. What were you looking for?"

"None of your business," said Joe simply. "The point is, what were you lookin' for?"

He was obviously not in a mood to be trifled with, so I told him.

"Did you find any black-headed pins to match up with the one you got?" he asked.

I shook my head. "I've been through all the bedrooms but this one and could not find any."

He walked to the door. "Next time you find a clue, leave it lay and call me, and don't waste your time runnin' around trying to find out what the clues mean. That's my job."

He went out and slammed the door, and I found I was shaking with helpless laughter. I went to the bureau for a handkerchief and had it in my hand when I noticed a packet of plain pins lying in the drawer. I picked it up and looked closely and saw that each pin had a black head.

CHAPTER
16

I STOOD FOR SOME minutes, turning the packet over in my hands and trying to remember where I had got it.

It came to me at last. It belonged to Mrs. Ballinger. She had been altering her lace dress two days before the arrival of the houseparty, and I had pinned it together for her to sew. I recalled that I had absentmindedly walked back to my room with the packet still in my hand and had thrown it into the drawer, intending to return it later.

I remembered, too, that when Mrs. Ballinger had sewed the dress she had removed the pins carefully and put them into a folding needlebook in her sewing basket. I dropped the packet back into the drawer and went straight to Mrs. Ballinger's room, where I was confronted by Joe and Richard. I stopped short and lost my poise to the extent of looking distinctly embarrassed.

Joe pinned me down with a suspicious stare. "Did you find them pins?"

I said, "Yes," meekly.

"Where?" he barked.

"In my bureau drawer," I said sheepishly.

Richard laughed heartily, but Joe was not amused and curtly requested him to shut up, after which he shoved his hands into his pockets and pinned me down again. "So you found them in your own room?"

I nodded uncomfortably, and Richard, who had been staring in mild astonishment at a photograph of Mrs. Ballinger's father, turned around and observed, "Nothing suspicious about that. After all, she came bounding in here the minute she found them to tell you about it."

"She came bounding in here all right," Joe agreed, "but not to tell me nothing. Nobody's gonna tell me that they come straight to the old dame's bedroom when they wanta find me. I'm a married man, and even if I wasn't, I got some pride."

Richard and I looked at each other, and then we both turned to stare at Joe, who chewed his toothpick unconcernedly.

"You're quite right, Joe," I said after a moment. "I did come here for something else, but I'm quite willing to tell you about it."

I explained about the pins, and the two of them watched while I went to Mrs. Ballinger's sewing basket and picked out the needlebook. The pins were there, and I started to count them carefully. I knew that I had used exactly one row in pinning the dress, and there had been none but the one row missing from the packet in my room.

There were two missing from Mrs. Ballinger's needlebook. One of them, of course, was still in the collar of my dressing gown.

"Musta lost the other while she was sewin' the dress," Joe observed.

I shook my head. "I'm sure it was not lost then. She's always careful about replacing pins. They cost money."

Joe thought it over. "But you had the whole packet salted away. Why didn't she raise hell about losin' that?"

"I told her I had them and promised to put them back. The next time she goes to her sewing basket she'll probably come flying to me in a fury about it."

Joe rested his bulk on the edge of a table and appeared to go into a brown study. Richard turned the photograph of Mrs. Ballinger's father to the wall and said idly, "I'd like to track down that last pin."

"Even Mrs. Ballinger loses things occasionally," I said doubtfully. "She might have dropped it somewhere, I suppose."

Joe evidently decided at this point to drop Mrs. Ballinger and the pins, for he said abruptly, "Now I wanta hear all about last night."

I told him everything that I could remember, and he listened closely.

"You say you locked both doors—the one to the hall, and the one to your room?"

"Yes."

"What did you do with the keys?"

"Why, I left them in the doors," I said faintly.

Joe just looked at me and shook his head in sorrow.

"Why didn't you lock up yourself, Joe?" Richard asked mildly.

"I wanted to, but the old dame was hollerin' out that somebody had to stay with the corpse all night, so when I left, this here Rosebud Hannahs was holdin' the fort."

"Well, it's obvious," Richard said, "that while we were drinking coffee in the kitchen, someone went through Leigh's room, brought Freda back, and arranged her in the chair. Someone with a rather ghoulish sense of humor."

It seemed a ripe time to ask Joe if I might move out of the house forthwith, but he answered my request with a curt "No," and his aspect was so forbidding that I let it drop without further ado. I did wonder if he had any legal right to keep me there and was inclined to think that he had not. I told him that I intended moving into Rhynda's bedroom, and he said, "All right," indifferently.

I went back to my room and started gathering my things together. I was not particularly anxious to make the change by that time, but Rhynda had reminded me of it, urgently, and had repeated that she could not stand being alone any longer. I made two or three trips with my various belongings, and when I had nearly finished I met Berg in the hall. He whispered to me that there was to be another conference in the small music room at four o'clock. It was just three-thirty then, so I nodded to him, and he went off.

I completed the arrangement of my things in Rhynda's room and then wandered downstairs to see if I could pick up any information from the gossipers. I went to the living room and found Mrs. Ballinger alone there. She had various brooms, dusters and mops lying about, and she was carrying an overstuffed chair from one side of the room to the other, her arms straining at it awkwardly. I went over and shouldered half the chair and helped her to set it down.

"I want no help from you, Leigh Smith," she said coldly.

I shrugged and left the room as silently as I had come. I thought that a little workout would do her no harm. I was pretty certain that she'd snap me up if I offered to return to my job a little later, and in the meantime, I was getting a nice rest. I went on to the large drawing room to see if the others were sitting in there.

They were not. Amy, surrounded by more brooms, dusters and mops, was trying to clean up and not making much headway. Her face had a streak of dirt and an expression of complete disgust. I lit a cigarette, leaned against the doorjamb, and watched her silently.

She looked up, pushed her hair back with a bent wrist, and said crossly, "Oh, for God's sake, go away."

I said, "No. I find it too interesting. It reminds me of my own early days as a skivvy."

"It wouldn't hurt you to help me."

"It would hurt my sense of justice," I explained kindly, "because I know you wouldn't help me if our positions were reversed."

She turned her back on me and set to work again, and after a minute or so she dropped an ashtray complete with butts onto a section of the carpet she had just cleaned. She stared at it in silent fury for a moment and then slowly stooped to pick it up.

I gave a refined little laugh. "Too bad. It's just those little things in housework that make it all so difficult."

She rose up and threw the ashtray straight at my head. It missed me, hit the doorframe, taking a chip out of it, and crashed to the floor in several pieces. I gazed at the fragments and clicked my tongue. "It cost five cents, too, and it will have to be replaced. Mrs. Ballinger will be upset."

"You don't have to tell her," Amy said quickly. "I'll get another one."

I nodded. "At the five, ten, fifteen and twenty-five cent store in the village. But tell me, Amy, what is this hold that Mrs. Ballinger has over you? It brings you to this dull uncomfortable place, throws a scare into you when Freda is on the point of telling her something about you, and actually has you wrestling with housework."

She looked me straight in the eye and said scornfully, "What do *you* think?"

I looked at her thoughtfully for a moment. "You surely don't think she has any money to leave, do you?"

"She has plenty," said Amy grimly. "Just because she's stingy doesn't mean she hasn't got it."

I thought she was making a mistake. I wondered if she had heard the story about Mrs. Ballinger having put all her money into insurance annuities which would stop at her death. I had supposed that all the nephews and nieces would know, since Freda had told me about it quite casually.

According to Freda, who had characterized the action as most selfish and inconsiderate, Mrs. Ballinger received quite a large monthly income from her annuities, of which she saved a considerable amount. She allowed this to accumulate for a time and then usually gave it to some charity or cause where her name would appear prominently. There would be nothing left for the relatives but the house itself. That was Freda's tale, and I was inclined to believe it.

I let it drop, however, for I had no proof of anything, and even if Amy were mistakenly exerting herself for nothing, I thought that a little housework would be good for her soul.

"What was the trouble concerning you and Freda and Donald Tait?" I asked after a while.

"None of your damned business," she snapped promptly.

"It is, as it happens," I said equably. "But I don't expect that to move you. Only, I want to know, and you can tell me—and Mrs. Ballinger would like to know certain things about you and Donald Tait—and I can tell her. So—"

"Oh, my God!" said Amy, in exasperation. "All this tittle-tattle! If it helps you any, Freda thought she was married to Donald."

CHAPTER
17

I STARED AT HER and did not realize that my mouth was hanging open until she said, "You don't look so bad that way. Your face is so naturally insipid that any sort of expression helps a bit."

I pulled myself together and said, "Oh well, an insipid face is a minor evil—better than being hideous, you know. You can always paint some glamour onto an insipid face, but it's awfully hard to paint off a nose or mouth, you know—?" I laughed brightly.

Amy never had much finesse. "If you're trying to tell me that I'm hideous—" she began angrily.

"Tell me what you mean about Freda," I interrupted.

She threw her duster away, sank down onto a chair, and pulled out a cigarette. I sat down near her.

"Start at the beginning," I said encouragingly.

"It's been a lot of stupid fuss about nothing. It all began last summer, when Freda and I were invited to a weekend houseparty. I knew Donald slightly at that time, and he was there, too."

"Well, is he really married? And was he married then?" I asked.

"Don't interrupt. Yes, of course. He's been married to Frances for years, but they don't go around together much any more."

I said, "Oh," and hoped I did not look like Rosalie Hannahs would have. Rosalie was determinedly sentimental about marriage.

"Was Frances at the houseparty?" I asked, getting in ahead of Amy, who had opened her mouth to continue.

"No, she wasn't there. For God's sake, let me finish this story, now that I've started it. Freda fell for Donald like a ton of bricks. Everybody noticed it, you couldn't help it. She didn't know he was married. In fact, she never knew. That time when she blurted out that he was married she thought it was to herself.

"The houseparty was pretty dull, the hostess being something like Freda, and we finally got so bored that we arranged a false elopement and marriage, with Freda as the heroine. Donald played up beautifully, and we had heaps of fun. He told Freda he had to leave on a trip immediately, and she swallowed it all.

"We never dreamed that she wouldn't realize sooner or later that it had all been a joke. But a couple of weeks later she saw us together in a restaurant, and she made a bit of a scene. Donald hates to be made conspicuous, and he always takes the easiest way out of a situation, anyhow, so he smoothed her down and told her he'd just got back and had run into me by accident. He said he had been going to phone her, and that it was very unfortunate but he had to leave town right away, again.

"She knew he was eeling, of course, but thought it was because I had stolen him away from her. She saw us together from time to time after that, and I guess she was dead sure by that time that I'd lured him from her.

"About a week before we came here, I told her the whole thing, explained that it was all a joke, and she wouldn't believe me—hardly listened. I told her again after we got here, and she called me a liar and worse.

"After that, she walked into Donald's room in the night, and he came flying into my room and locked the connecting door. She stayed there until early morning, not making a sound, and then went back to her own room."

"And then Donald went back to his own room," I said nastily.

"He'd been sitting on a straight chair all the time," she declared belligerently. "He was frozen stiff."

I felt faintly sick when I thought of Freda. I knew she must have suffered badly through the whole thing, but Amy was the sort who never thought or cared about the suffering of a girl like Freda.

I remembered the night she had slipped into Donald's room and thought uncomfortably of the humiliation she must have felt. Since she had not tried to call to him through the door, she must have decided at once that it was no use. Evidently she had stood at the door waiting for a chance to return to her own room unobserved by the deputy in the hall.

I sighed and glanced at my watch. To my surprise, it read a quarter past four, and I stood up hastily. I considered explaining to Amy that she was a mean pig and realized immediately that it would be worse than useless.

I left her sitting dispiritedly among her brooms and dusters and went along to the small music room. Berg and Richard were already there, and I could hear them talking heatedly. They stopped abruptly when I appeared. I dropped into a chair and looked from one to the other.

"What's the argument?"

Richard smiled at me guilelessly, and Berg's face was innocent surprise and gentle denial. "No argument," he lied.

I looked them over coldly. "Either you spill it, or you won't hear one word of what I was going to tell you."

"Smithy," said Richard reproachfully, "you sound exactly like Joe."

"And you're fifteen minutes late," Berg added.

I pulled out a cigarette, and they jumped together and held two lights for it.

I slumped in my chair, puffed unconcernedly, and studied my shoes.

"Stubborn little mule," said Berg resignedly. "I was merely telling Dick that he ought to stay away from Rhynda just now, for a decent interval, anyway."

I had a fleeting regret that I had made them tell me, and I continued to slump in my chair, feeling oddly depressed. I pulled myself together after a minute and said nobly, "Rhynda needs a friend now, and someone a bit more strong than Rosalie Hannahs."

"*I'll* take care of Rhynda," Berg declared impatiently.

"Nearest male relative," I murmured and tried not to smile. But I wondered a little if all this trouble were not toning Berg down a bit and perhaps making a man of him.

I remembered my intention of getting in touch with Rhynda's people and thought that it was quite possible Berg was not the nearest male relative. I made up my mind to see to it directly our conference was over. I told them Amy's story, and they both made ungentlemanly comments about Amy and Donald Tait.

"I suppose it isn't possible that Tait disposed of Freda because she was becoming too much of a nuisance?" Richard suggested, without conviction.

Berg shook his head. "He'd hardly resort to anything as desperate as that. And what about John?"

Richard shrugged. "Unless Freda had confided in John, and John had threatened Tait."

"No," said Berg, with finality. "It must be someone who knows this house well, and Tait has never been here before. How could he fix up that contraption in the attic?"

"What contraption?" Richard asked.

Berg sighed. "I wish we knew. I've searched the attic until there can't be a square inch left, and I can't find anything. But there must be a contraption somewhere—there has to be— and I want to be in the attic when it performs again.

"I think you may be right, Dick, about a high wind being necessary before it can be worked, and I'd like you to come to the attic with me the next time we have any wind. I have a hunch that I'm supposed to go next—the only Ballinger left, and all that—but I intend to put up a fight. They may get me, but they're not going to get me easily." He seemed quite fierce about it.

"I think you're barking up the wrong tree," Richard said easily. "What could anyone gain by killing the three of you? My guess is that they were after John, and that Freda saw something, as she said, and was killed for that reason."

"Perhaps," Berg said vaguely. He turned to me. "Didn't you get anything out of her last night?"

"Nothing. I think she knew I was trying to pump her, and she simply closed up."

We were all silent for a space, and then Berg asked, "What is Joe doing, in his blundering way?"

"Joe," said Richard firmly, "has fewer hayseeds on him than you might suppose."

"Sarcasm?" Berg suggested.

"Simple truth. I've worked with Joe, and it's a pleasure. He never misses a trick."

Berg glanced at me, and we both smiled skeptically.

"He intends to have this thing cleared up by tomorrow noon at the latest," Richard continued, "because, according to him, some interfering lice are coming to assist him if he doesn't."

"I should think he'd be glad to have assistance," I said.

"Well, he has his pride," Richard explained, "and, of course, he has me, too."

"If that's all he has," said Berg loftily, "it's high time he got some help from the lice."

I found myself buttoning my sweater up to the chin and realized that I was getting chilly. I glanced around at the window and saw that it was rattling a bit and that the curtains were swaying gently.

"Wind!" I exclaimed and looked at the other two expectantly.

Richard got up and looked out into the twilight. "There is a bit of wind. If it really blows up, Berg, we'll spend the evening in the attic." He turned to me. "No one is to know we're there. Will you see to it, Leigh?"

"I'll do my best," I promised.

"Don't bother about your best, Smithy," said Berg. "Just make *certain* that nobody knows."

I gave him a scornful glance and pulled out a cigarette. He followed suit, and Richard produced a pipe, which he managed to light after using six matches on it.

We sat and smoked in silence for some time. I had almost finished my cigarette when the closet door beside me suddenly burst open. We all jumped and stared—and as we looked, Joe emerged. He did not so much as glance at us but stalked out of the room in grim silence.

CHAPTER
18

WE LOOKED AT each other in consternation, and then Richard began to laugh. "He waited for us to leave, until he couldn't stand it any longer."

"Hiding out to hear our confidences," Berg said. "but how did he know that we were going to meet here?"

"I told you that he never misses a trick," Richard reminded us. "Joe is a born snoop and that's how he holds his job. He always knows who people are and what they're doing."

"If you're going to the attic you'd better go now," I told them. "You'll certainly have Joe in amongst you. He's probably waiting for you."

They agreed to go at once and decided to come downstairs for dinner so that no one would ask about their activities. My job was to make sure that their absence was not particularly noticed. We parted company, and I went upstairs to tidy myself for dinner.

I was fixing up my face when I heard a banging and clattering outside the house. I went to the window, raised it, looked out, and was appalled to discover that the fuel company from the village was delivering coal and logs. I knew that we were not supposed to order coal until January the eleventh, exactly, and the logs were pure, superfluous luxury.

After my first gasp, I remembered that I had not yet been re-hired and began to giggle. I threw on a wrap and went down to show the men where to stack the logs, and which cellar window to use for the coal chute. I indicated the spot for the logs first and then went outside while they inserted the chute in the window.

I realized uneasily that I was standing at just about the place where John had fallen. My eyes sought the ground involuntarily, and in the square of light from one of the ground floor windows, I noticed a faint glitter. I stooped and stretched my hand for it. It was a plain pin, with a black head. I turned it uncertainly in my fingers for a moment and then stuck it in my dress and went quickly into the house.

I met Rosalie Hannahs in the hall. "Who ordered the coal?" I asked.

She said, "Miss Perrin," as though the name brought on a bad taste in her mouth.

"How on earth did she get them to deliver it on Sunday?"

"I believe she told them that we were quite out of fuel, and that there was someone suffering from pneumonia in the house. Lies seem to come easily to her." She compressed her lips and gave the impression that the bad taste was getting worse.

Mrs. Ballinger sailed into the hall, and I tried to get away, but Rosalie caught me firmly by the arm. "Miss Smith and I were discussing Miss Perrin's propensity for lies," she said sweetly.

Mrs. Ballinger glanced at me through narrowed lids. She was always quite free with criticism for her relatives herself, but I knew she resented it coming from anyone else. "I can't see that Amy tells more lies than the average young woman," she said coldly.

I tried to slip away again at this point to avoid the row, but Rosalie hung onto me and headed straight into it.

"Well!" she said stiffly. "She just told a most appalling lie to the coal company."

Mrs. Ballinger reared like a startled horse. Coal company meant "Bill," and it was not yet January the eleventh. "What was Amy saying to them?" she asked excitedly. "We had no reason to communicate with them."

"Why, she was ordering coal and logs, of course," Rosalie said innocently.

"How dare she do such a thing!" Mrs. Ballinger thundered, her face a dark mottled red. She had barely got the words out of her mouth when the culprit walked out of the parlor, dragging a mop behind her. Mrs. Ballinger pounced and roared.

"Amy! What do you mean by ordering coal and logs for this house? You shall pay for it out of your own pocket, make no mistake about that."

Amy gave her an evil look, and after a moment's hesitation, said aggressively, "You needn't try and blame me for all the things that were bought yesterday. Richard Jones is responsible for every last one of them, and I understood him to say he was paying for them, too." She disappeared hastily in the direction of the kitchen.

Mrs. Ballinger stared after her as long as she was visible and then turned to stare at Rosalie and me. "What does she mean? What is she talking about? What was bought yesterday? I will not have people buying things without asking me about it."

"I guess she means all the groceries that were delivered yesterday," Rosalie said soothingly.

"Groceries!"

"And liquors. Several cases, I believe. I thought it was so considerate of you when you don't drink yourself."

Mrs. Ballinger turned on me, and in a voice of death demanded that I get Richard Jones at once and deliver him to her.

I said, "Certainly" and made for the stairs. I had no intention of seeking out Richard, but I wanted to escape from the fuss.

I went to Mrs. Ballinger's room first and matched the pin I had picked up with those in her needlebook. They were the same, and there was none missing. I went back to my old room and counted the pins in the packet which I had left in the bureau drawer when I moved my things. None was missing there, either, so that now I had them all. And one had been found on the floor of the bathroom closet after Freda had died, and one on the ground where John had fallen. I stood and stared at them, wondering what they meant.

There was a smart rap on the door, and before I had time to say anything it was flung open, and Richard walked in.

"Sold again!" he said, looking disappointed.

"Anything wrong?" I asked quickly.

"Well, I had hoped to catch you in your undies."

"Nobody," I said grimly, "is going to catch me in the undies I am forced to wear in this house."

He laughed, stretched himself out on the bed, and lighted a cigarette. "Then you got me in here under false pretenses."

"Mrs. Ballinger is looking for you," I said warningly. "Amy blamed you for all the stuff she ordered Saturday and is probably going to blame you for the coal and logs that came today. Mrs. B. wants your head on a platter."

"She'll have to wait her turn," he said idly. "I'm very careful to divide my time equally among my lady friends."

"It makes us all very happy," I said graciously. "It's just those little things that mean so much to a woman."

He transferred his gaze from the ceiling to the packet of pins that I still held in my hand. "It isn't always easy, you know, to give the full quota. For instance now, knowing that you stand there with red flannels under your dress—" He folded his arm under his head and continued to look at the packet. "Have you, perhaps, found the final pin?"

I nodded. "I'm going to hand it over to Joe and tell him all. I'm afraid of Joe."

He sat up abruptly and disposed of his cigarette. "Where did you find it?"

"Perhaps I'd better tell you some other time. Your duty to the other ladies, you know?"

"I'll square it with them this evening. Go on, Smithy, and remember all details."

I told him all about it, and he listened with deep attention. He took the pin I had found and looked at it, and it flashed in his hand as he held it up to the light.

"A nice bright new pin," he murmured obscurely.

There was a rustle at the door, and it swung open to reveal Mrs. Ballinger. She looked at Richard, still seated on the bed, and then at me, resting my elbows on the footboard. I think she had expected the situation to be more compromising but felt that a rebuke was in order anyway. "Leigh! I thought better of you—really! This is your bedroom."

"Not any more," I said. "I'm sleeping in with Rhynda from now on."

"With Rhynda?" she repeated vaguely. Her eyes slipped about the room and came to rest on Richard. "You're old enough to know better, young man. If you want to talk to one of the girls, there are plenty of public rooms."

"Still," said Richard, in a mildly argumentative tone, "one must be chivalrous, and Smithy prefers privacy when she proposes marriage to me. I prefer it myself, too, because I haven't made up my mind about accepting her yet. I want to be *sure*, you know, such a serious step—"

Mrs. Ballinger's mouth fell open, and she looked at me rather helplessly.

"Silly liar," I said. "He's dying to accept, but he can't get his mother's consent, and he's afraid to go ahead without."

Mrs. Ballinger began to scent banter and closed her mouth with a snap. "You ought to be ashamed of yourself, Leigh, talking like that when you have a fine man like Berg."

"*I* have Berg?" I said in amazement.

"You don't have to pretend with me," she said crossly. "I know all about it. He wanted that diamond ring, the old one that belonged to my husband's mother, but I told him that no bride would care for an old ring. It's better to buy a new one, even if it has to be very small."

Richard stood up abruptly. "Are you telling me that Berg wants to marry Leigh?" he demanded.

"Yes, certainly."

"Well, he forgot to tell me," I said. "And he'd have to show me a bit more attention before I'd believe it, anyway."

"How could he pay you attention at a time like this?" Mrs. Ballinger snorted. "With all he's been through!"

I sighed and shook my head. "Even so, I'm afraid I can't believe it. If Berg is in love with me, then Joe is, too."

"Me?" said Joe's horrified voice, and he stepped in behind Mrs. Ballinger.

"Well, aren't you?" I asked, putting on one of Amy's provocative pouts.

"No," said Joe shortly. "I told you once, I'm a married man."

"She has her points, though," Richard suggested. "Pretty, don't you think?"

"No," Joe said simply. "I like a woman to have dark hair and light eyes, and she oughta be properly upholstered. This one has light hair and dark eyes." He glanced at me and went on with a certain amount of emotion, "And Jeez! What a figure! Looks as if she hadn't bad a square meal in a month." He half closed his eyes and added reminiscently, "Although I know different."

Mrs. Ballinger made a vexed sound with her tongue. "You've no call to say that. Leigh is a trifle too thin but she is far from looking starved."

"She's far from being starved, too," said Joe and unexpectedly gave voice to a loud guffaw.

Mrs. Ballinger waited, frowning, for him to subside. When quiet was restored, she looked at her watch and said, "Dinner will be ready in five minutes, and I came here to tell you that we are going to hold a seanc, directly after dinner. I will not put up with what has been going on in this house any longer. Luckily, Mrs. Hannahs tells me she is a medium—has those powers anyway—so that we should be able to find out from John and Freda themselves what this is all about. And I know they will tell us that their deaths were accidental. There's no use denying it. We received the warnings, and the accidents followed." She turned to leave. "You may attend the seance, too," she said graciously to Joe and took herself off.

"Thanks for nothin'," said Joe coldly. "I was comin' anyway." He turned to me. "What are you doing with them pins?"

I told him about my discovery meekly enough, and he examined the packet and the pin I had found. After that, we had to march back to Mrs. Ballinger's room while he looked at the needlebook again.

I got it out of the sewing basket, and we counted the pins carefully—only this time there were two missing.

CHAPTER
19

WE MUST HAVE COUNTED those pins six or seven times, but the result was always the same, and at last we gave up and just looked at each other.

"But they were here a few minutes ago," I said helplessly. "I came in and counted them, and there was not one missing. Not more than fifteen minutes ago, I'm sure."

Joe shrugged, and Richard said slowly, "If you are sure they were here at that time, then someone came and took them while you were in the other room. But I'm damned if I know why."

Joe grunted and began to search through the sewing basket to see if the pins had fallen out of the needlebook, but there was no sign of them. He gave up at last and, taking the pin I had found outside, wrapped it up and put it away in his pocket. We went down to dinner, and on the way I asked Richard about the attic.

"We did go up," he said, "but the wind died right away again, so we came down."

"Well, but are you sure the thing works only when there is a wind?"

"No," he admittecl. "We can't be sure. It's only a possibility. But we can't sit up there all the time."

Everyone was at the table when we got down, and there was a place laid for Joe. We milled around a bit and got ourselves seated, and I found that I was between Berg and Amy. Amy had put herself beside Donald Tait again, and Mrs. Ballinger either had not noticed or no longer cared. Fighting something out with Amy was a pretty wearing business.

After we had finished the meal, Mrs. Ballinger announced that as soon as Doris had cleared the table we would return for the seance, and she added firmly that she wanted everyone to be present.

Joe heard her through and then took the floor himself to inform us that we would all be expected to attend the inquest on the following day. We shifted to the living room, and Richard, lagging behind with Berg and me, spoke to us in a rapid undertone.

"The autopsy on Freda showed that the blow only stunned her and that she was actually drowned in the bathtub. Her nightgown had a small bloodstain on the neck, and they think she was hit before the gown was removed and that it was stained as it was pulled over her head. Lawyer says Mrs. B. leaves nothing but house and personal effects. Trust fund reverts to you, Berg, Rhynda is out of it, and Mrs. B. inherits if you go."

Berg muttered, "God! They'll arrest me before morning!"

I left them and went to pour coffee, and Mrs. Ballinger immediately came to grips with Richard.

"I understand you ordered coal and logs and intend to pay for them."

Richard looked at her speculatively. "I didn't order them, as it happens, but I know who did, and I'll keep it dark for a consideration. As for the fuel, I'll pay the bill, which ought to be more than adequate for my room and board for the week."

Mrs. Ballinger, who had been ready for a lively battle, colored uncomfortably and seemed a bit at a loss. I could see that she was afraid to tell him that he need not pay for fear he would take her at her word, and on the other hand, she could hardly say, "Thank you" to a guest for offering to pay his board. Her greediness for money often put her into embarrassing situations, and I watched with interest to see how she'd squirm out of it. To my disappointment, she was spared the necessity, for at that moment Rhynda spilled her coffee and it streamed down the front of Berg's suit.

Berg jumped and exclaimed, and the cup crashed to the floor. "Hadn't you heard that I'm out of a job?" he asked humorously. "This suit was supposed to last five or ten years."

Rhynda was usually quick with her tongue, and we were all surprised when, instead of answering him in kind, she began quietly to cry. Rosalie hurried over to pat her hand and murmur soothingly to her, and Berg tilted up her face and mopped at her wet eyes with his handkerchief.

"You weren't supposed to cry," he said reprovingly. "I was trying to be funny."

She smiled faintly then, and Berg went upstairs to change. We finished our coffee, and then Richard gave me a sign, and I slipped out and upstairs. Richard followed me, and we went along to Berg's room. Berg opened the door and ushered us in.

"What about the attic?" Richard asked, without preamble. "We can't sit up there and be among those present at the seance too."

Berg said slowly, "I'm sure that noise is worked by hand, Dick, and since everyone will be in the dining room, I don't expect it to start up."

"You don't think the wind has anything to do with it, then?"

Berg shook his head. "I've come to the conclusion that it's just coincidence."

"You may be right," Richard said, without conviction, "but if there is anything in the wind theory, we shouldn't miss out on it tonight. Listen to it."

I had not particularly noticed it before, but when Berg and I stopped to listen, I realized uneasily that the wind was howling and shrieking around the house. I looked at them with widened eyes, and Berg took a restless turn about the room. "It's a honey," he said, after a minute. "I suppose we shouldn't pass it up."

We went out into the hall and stood uncertainly at the foot of the attic stairs.

"Well, let's go down and start the seance," Berg suggested, "and after they've put the lights out, we can creep up quietly. Aunt Mabel keeps the lights out for at least two hours during these affairs. Leigh can stay and let us know what goes on. When the thing is nearly over, she can sneak out and tell us, and we can sneak back to our places."

"Too much sneaking," I protested. "Somebody's going to get

caught. Besides, how on earth am I to know when the thing is nearly over?"

"Easy," said Berg. "Aunt Mabel always runs the proceedings, no matter who acts as medium, and when it's over, she insists that the sitters remain in silence with all lights out for at least fifteen minutes, so that the spirits can depart with all dignity."

"All right," I said reluctantly, "but I really don't see the sense of you two sitting up there, when everyone else is down in the dining room."

"It's a good chance to tear the attic apart," Richard said, "without someone meddling in. And if it is something that depends upon the wind alone, we ought to be able to find it."

We went down to the dining room. Mrs. Ballinger was very impatient to begin, and the lights were put out immediately. We fumbled our way to seats around the dining table and were told to hold hands. It was difficult to reach each other, and I felt sure that someone would comment on it and the absence of Berg and Richard would be noticed. However, we managed it finally and settled down. I had Rosalie on one side of me and Joe on the other.

I have found that the trouble with seances is that it takes so long for anything to happen, and this one was no exception. It took Rosalie, our medium, about ten minutes to work herself into the state of imagination where she could believe that the spirits were talking through her. I moved my stiff body cautiously and thought that at least we would get Rosalie's version of the affair. The time seemed interminable, and I had just got to the point where I was considering giving Joe's hand a loving little squeeze when Mrs. Ballinger spoke.

"I want to speak to my beloved nephew, John," she said solemnly.

Rosalie started to tremble and then called, in a high, squeaky voice, "John! John! Where are you, John?"

I was tempted to answer, "Here," in deep bass, but Rosalie got in first and answered herself.

"I am here," she said, several octaves lower.

"Darling John," Mrs. Ballinger said, evidently in tears. "We miss you so. It's been such a shock. So dreadful. But we must know how you died, what sort of accident, how it happened. Please tell us." She faltered and ended up in a burst of sentimentality, "For the sake of your little, unborn son."

There was a moment of dead silence, and then the low voice said distinctly, "The unborn child is not mine."

CHAPTER
20

THERE WAS A commotion, and I heard a chair pushed back and some-one get up, while Amy's strident laughter rang out. Light flooded the room, and after a preliminary blinking, I saw that Rhynda was stand-ing by the door, flushed and trembling.

"If you meant that as a joke, Rosalie Hannahs," she said furi-ously, "it's in very poor taste."

Rosalie, trying owlishly to focus her eyes in the sudden light, looked both astonished and uneasy. "Why, Rhynda," she said unhap-pily, "it had nothing to do with me, dear. You know I could never say such a thing."

"Don't be a damned fool!" Rhynda snapped. "Do you think we're a bunch of children? I've a good mind to sue you for libel!" She left the room, and we could hear her running up stairs.

Rosalie shook her head and looked around at us with a hurt expression.

"Are you sure it was John speaking?" Mrs. Ballinger asked un-comfortably.

"Absolutely. It was John," Rosalie declared firmly.

"But you actually said the words?" I asked.

"Yes. But, of course, I'm only the medium. The spirits speak through me and use my voice."

"We must go on," said Mrs. Ballinger. "We must find out more, and I shall ask John if it is really true about the baby. I can't believe it."

We sat down again, and Joe changed his place and sat on Rosalie's other side, which left me sitting between Rosalie and Donald Tait. With Rhynda out, we had to stretch our arms so that we were hold-ing onto each other by the tips of our fingers. We sat in silence for a while, and then Mrs. Ballinger asked for John again.

Rosalie didn't waste any time. She answered at once, "I'm here," in the same low voice.

"John," said Mrs Ballinger agitatedly, "tell me truly, is Rhynda's child not yours?"

"Not mine," said the voice promptly.

Mrs. Ballinger sighed heavily, hesitated, and then asked how he had died.

"I cannot say."

She became a bit impatient with spirit John at this point. "But can't you tell us? You *must* say something, give us some hint?"

There was a pause, and then, "Look inside the old piano."

The sitters stirred, and there was a sort of wordless wave of satisfaction. We seemed to be getting somewhere.

"Give us more hints, John," Mrs. Ballinger said eagerly.

There was a much longer pause, and I felt sure Rosalie had told all she knew. Finally she sighed and said, "I cannot tell you any more."

"But, John, please!" Mrs. Ballinger said tensely. "Give us one more message, just one."

Dead silence, this time, and it lasted so long that I could not hold myself in any longer. I imitated Rosalie's low voice and said, "Please give Leigh Smith a thousand dollars."

Rosalie jumped up at once, and Mrs. Ballinger must have done so, too, because when the light went on she was standing by the switch. She looked thunder at me, and I gazed back at her in round-eyed astonishment.

Rosalie remarked that it was a pity we had so much levity to contend with and that she did not think John would return again tonight. Undoubtedly he was offended.

"Then that last bit was not John speaking?" Mrs. Ballinger asked, wanting to make sure of it.

"Oh no, no. John was quite silent."

"On the contrary," I said, "he spoke through me. My powers as a medium—"

"Rubbish, Leigh!" said Mrs. Ballinger shortly. "You're not a medium." She turned away from me and began to make arrangements with Rosalie for another seance the following night with only the right people present. In the midst of it she noticed the absence of Berg and Richard, and at the same moment I realized that Joe was no longer with us. I slipped out of the door and dashed across to the little music room.

Joe was standing by the piano, holding a small hammer with his pocket handkerchief wrapped around it. I recognized it as one we had kept in one of the bathroom cupboards for small repair jobs upstairs. He glanced up at me and said, "I been waiting for youse."

"How did you know I was coming?"

"You ain't called Nosey Smith for nothin'," he explained matter-of-factly.

"Who called me Nosey Smith?" I demanded, incensed.

"I did," he said calmly. "Now, I want to know about this here hammer. Does it belong in the house, and where was it kept?"

"It belongs to the house, and it was kept in the bathroom. Where did you find it? In the piano?"

"What do you think?" he asked disgustedly.

The lid of the piano was open, and I peeped in and saw that there was a space large enough for the hammer, but it looked as though it would have to rest against the harp, so that if anyone were playing there would be a sour note every now and then. I figured that Rosalie was the type to tinkle out ditties on the piano and noticed the sour notes, and so discovered the hammer.

"But why did she keep quiet about it?" I said aloud. "Why didn't she go around asking why there should be a hammer in the piano?"

"She probably hauled it out and found it was bloodstained, and then, I figger, she dropped it back in a hurry," Joe observed.

I turned sharply and looked at the hammer. The head was darkly stained, and I shuddered.

"What is it?" I whispered.

"Well," said Joe easily, "puttin' two and two together, I would say it was the weapon used on the Freda dame." I closed my eyes and turned my head away. "I'm goin' to get the fingerprints on it," he added confidently.

"They'll be Rosalie's, mostly."

"I'll have to take that into account," he admitted. "Now I'm gain' up to the attic and see how them two G-men are makin' out."

I had forgotten Richard and Berg for the moment. "How did you know they were in the attic?" I asked curiously.

"By puttin' two and two together," he said, and walked out of the room.

I ran after him and followed him to the kitchen, where he handed the hammer over to Doris,with instructions to deliver it to one of his deputies who was due to arrive in half an hour. He went on up the back stairs, and I trailed close behind him. When we got to the second floor, we found the hall in total darkness. We fumbled our way to the switch, but when we turned it on there was still no light.

"Bulb's broke," said Joe's voice. "I'll get another. Where do you keep them?"

I laughed shortly. "You'll have to take one out of another socket. There are no extras in this house."

He swore softly and made his way to the bathroom, where he turned on the light and left the door open so that we could see our way to the attic stairs. He led the way up, and I followed him.

Richard and Berg were playing vingt-et-un by the light of a candle. "Any luck?" Joe asked.

"Right out," said Richard bitterly. "I've lost three dollars."

Joe said, "Hell! Do you want me to burst out cryin'? I mean any luck with that draggin' noise?"

Berg yawned and scooped up the cards. "Nothing at all. How did the seance go?"

Joe lowered himself onto a wooden packing box, and pulling a battered cigarette from his pocket, lighted it at the candle.

"We been informed that Mrs. John Ballinger is goin' to have a baby that don't, rightly speaking, belong to her late husband."

Berg stood up, and the line of his jaw grew rigid. "That's going beyond a joke. Whoever said it will retract and apologize."

Joe inhaled nearly half his cigarette and let it out slowly. "That ain't going to be so easy, son. It was the spook of the late Mr. John Ballinger that spilled the dirt."

"Never mind that rubbish," Berg said impatiently. "Who actually said it?"

"Mrs. Hannahs was the one who give it voice." I had an idea that Joe was amused.

"That one!" Berg muttered through his teeth.

I remembered again about Rhynda's relatives and that I had twice intended to try and get in touch with some of them and had entirely forgotten it each time. I spared a moment of regret for my faulty memory; it wasn't very nice for Rhynda to have things like this going around.

"Youse guys gonna stay up here all night?" Joe asked.

"Not me," Richard said definitely. "I'm going to bed."

"I suppose I'd only fall asleep if I stayed," Berg said reluctantly.

"How about Smithy and Joe doing a stretch?" Richard suggested. "They seem to be keeping steady company."

Joe colored angrily. "Listen," he shouted, "you got no call to start any scandal about me. My wife wouldn't like it, and it ain't my fault if this spindle-legged kid follows me around."

"No, it ain't," said Richard.

Berg laughed and tucked my hand through his arm. "Come on, Smithy, we'll go and have some light refreshments. I didn't have much dinner and I'm hungry. I'm one man you don't have to tag after to get."

"That's my fiancee you're walking off with," Richard called.

"No, I ain't," I said.

"This will mean pistols, Ballinger," Richard shouted, raising his voice as we descended the stairs. "And you, Smithy—you have a care."

We got down to the second-floor hall and found that it was in total darkness again. I explained to Berg that the bulb must be broken, and we groped our way to the bathroom and turned the light on there.

"I guess Mrs. Ballinger found it burning after Joe and I left," I said. "She probably has it figured out that the hall light will have to stay dark until enough electricity has been saved to pay for a new bulb."

He looked down at me and chuckled, but his eyes were tired and strained. "Keep chattering, Smithy. Don't stop, and don't mention this ghastly business. I want to get my mind away from it."

"I'll talk your ear off," I promised. "Only go on down now and put the kettle on. I want to wash my hands."

He went off, and after I had washed I went along to my former room, intending to tidy my hair. I did not remember about the change until I had gone in and turned on the light. The bare room reminded me, and I had turned impatiently to go out when something unusual about the bedside table stopped me. It took me a moment to realize that it was a telephone, the old extension that had been in Mrs. Ballinger's bedroom and that she had had disconnected because it cost about fifty cents a month. It had been pushed away into a corner of the shelf in her bedroom closet, and she had said once or twice that she intended putting it away in the attic.

It stood now, with the severed wires wound neatly around its base, on my bedside table.

CHAPTER
21

I STOOD AND LOOKED at that dusty old telephone, and shaking my head slowly, reflected that the place was certainly a madhouse. What possible reason could there be for anyone to bring the thing from Mrs. Ballinger's closet and put it there on the table? It seemed unlikely that Mrs. Ballinger herself would do it, for it was not her way to leave things lying around, not because she was naturally tidy, but because things left lying about might be stolen.

I gave it up with a shrug and turned to leave the room when I caught sight of Rosalie's leather shopping list, which I had used to write down the peculiar things I had found in the various bedrooms. I picked it up and took it along with me.

In Rhynda's room I tucked the shopping list under the pillow on my bed and then went to the bureau to brush my hair. Rhynda was sitting up in bed, reading. She marked the place in her book with a wisp of embroidered handkerchief, shivered a little in her shell-pink velvet bedjacket, and asked, "What other lies did that bitch Rosalie tell about me after I left?"

"She didn't say anything more about you. In fact, she pretty well shut up altogether."

"She'd better shut up, as far as I'm concerned," Rhynda said ominously. "I'll sue her."

"So you should," I agreed, intent on my hair. "It's a mean, underhanded sort of way to gossip—Rosalie's method."

"But it isn't true!" she flared.

"No, no, of course not," I said hastily. "It was unfortunate, though, because I think Mrs. Ballinger drank it all in as gospel. She's a great believer in the spirits."

"Mrs. Mabel Stinkpot Ballinger is a stingy, greedy old hag and can go straight to hell as far as I am concerned," Rhynda said firmly.

I wanted to go and shake her by the hand but decided against it as being too sentimental. However, I told her that I agreed with her wholeheartedly, and after a final pat at my hair, I left the room to go to my supper with Berg.

The bathroom light was still on and the door open, so that I could see my way to the stairs easily enough. The lower hall was dimly lighted, as usual, and I wended my way through the various doors and back hall until I made the kitchen.

My mind had been on Rhynda since I had left her bedroom. It seemed to me that her nervous, hysterical condition had changed and that she was suddenly calm and almost unconcerned. I wondered if something had happened, or if it were merely Time, the Great Healer.

Berg was munching an apple. The kettle was on, but there were no other preparations.

"Playing the helpless man?" I asked, raising my eyebrows. "You ought to see Jonesy in the kitchen."

"I did what you told me to," he said between bites. "Anyway, I had a nagging suspicion that you were delaying up there so that I'd have it all done. Maybe you can fool that chump Dick, but I'm made of sterner stuff."

I made up a tasty little supper, and we sat down at the kitchen table to eat it. Berg ate for a while in silence, and then he said suddenly, "You know, I think I'm getting somewhere, at last. I believe, well, I think I'm going to be able to untangle it."

"What is it?" I asked breathlessly.

He grinned at me and shook his head. "Nope. Can't tell."

"Why not?" I demanded. "I think that's mean. I tell you everything as it comes along."

"Keep your hair on, Smithy. I'll tell you just as soon as I'm sure I'm right. I can't now, because there's always the possibility that I'm wrong. I'll know soon, though, and then I'll tell you."

I sighed impatiently and picked up my fork again.

"Mad?" he asked, putting on his most charming smile.

I said, "Yes," and jammed some herring into my mouth.

"Are you going to leave the old lady when this is all over?" he asked presently.

"I guess so. I haven't really saved enough money, but somehow, I can't stand her or the house much longer."

"Don't blame you. Listen, Smithy, will you go out with me when we get back to New York?"

"Oh, I guess so, if you want."

"Overwhelming enthusiasm," he murmured.

I put on a wide grin. "I'll be so *happy* to go out with you when we get back to New York, Bergie."

He laughed and said, "That'll be enough lip from you, you undersized little runt."

I poured fresh coffee for us, and for a while we ate in silence. Then Berg said, with apparent irrelevance, "I've got to do *something* to take my mind off the thing."

"Even like taking me out in New York?"

"Not as uncomplimentary as it sounds," he said, without smiling. "It takes a good deal to divert me just now."

We finished our supper shortly after that and turned all the lights out and went upstairs. By this time, as I had expected, the bathroom light was off again, and after we had switched off the dim light in the lower hall, we could not have seen our hands before our faces.

We groped our way along, laughing a little, until we came to Berg's door. He dropped a light kiss on my face, which happened to land on my nose, and whispered, "I'm going straight to bed—I'm all in. Haven't slept for two nights, and if I don't get some real rest I'll be too groggy to do anything. I don't think that damned noise will start up as long as someone is up there."

"Well, but is anyone up there?" I asked doubtfully.

"Dick and Joe may still be there. I know Dick's going to bed eventually, but Joe hasn't confided his plans to me. I don't think it will help him much if he does stay, because he always goes to sleep when his bedtime comes, even if he's standing on his feet."

I giggled. "How do you know?"

"Doris told me, but she went on to admit, grudgingly, that he was so good in the daytime that he always got his man, anyway."

I laughed as silently as I could and started to feel my way along to the bathroom. I found the switch after a certain amount of fumbling, and as light flooded the room I jumped and gasped audibly. Joe was sitting on a chair in the middle of the floor. He blinked and looked at me with profound disgust.

"Do you intend to spend the night here?" I asked mildly. "Because it's going to be a bit inconvenient."

"I thought you was all in bed," he said, getting up. "I forgot how you always have to go down and feed your face when you oughta be sleepin'." He seemed thoroughly put out.

I glanced over my shoulder and saw that Berg was still in the hall. I could see his grin in the light that shone from the bathroom.

"I'm sorry," I said feebly. "I suppose you were waiting to pounce on someone, and we spoiled it all."

"Oh hell," said Joe. "Everybody's got their own troubles, and you're mine. I'm goin' down and get something to eat, supposin' you've left anything."

He went away, and Berg stepped into the light, still grinning. "It's a trap. I don't believe he's gone downstairs at all. He's probably going to sit in one of the rooms and wait for us to get on with our dirty work so that he can catch us at it."

We laughed together, and I thought briefly that Berg was beginning to be more like his old self. We started down the hall to our rooms, but when we got abreast of Richard's door it was suddenly flung open, and he stood on the threshold in a dressing robe of royal purple.

He looked us up and down. "Oh," he said, "it's youse. Well, I'm going to complain to the management. Incessant whispering and laughing and carrying on all night. A guy can't sleep. And then, mind you, it turns out to be my best friend, cavorting with my best girl. Bad cess to the two of you."

"You shouldn't have left your post in the attic," I pointed out. "I expect you could have slept there undisturbed."

He drew himself up. "Madam," he began, and at that moment Mrs. Ballinger's door started to open. "Cheese it," he ended urgently.

Berg and I pushed him back into his room and piled in after him. We listened, with our ears against the door, and heard Mrs. Ballinger come out into the hall.

"Who is there, please?" she called.

We remained quiet, and after a moment she repeated her question. Then she started to walk away, but instead of going back into her room, she went straight downstairs.

"Poor Joe," said Berg sadly. "He's down there eating her food."

"I'll back Joe," I said promptly, "if you want to make any bets."

Richard stepped between us. "Don't think you can continue your nonsense in here, because you can't. Just kiss me good night and go."

"Go on, Berg," I said. "He wants to be kissed."

Berg shuffled his feet and murmured bashfully, "Aw, shucks! I think he means you."

"Then he's out of luck. I'm engaged to Joe. We're only waiting for the divorce."

"For God's sake, Smithy," said Richard pitifully, "go to bed just this once, to see how it feels, and let me get some sleep."

I opened the door and peered out, and as far as I could see, the hall was empty. I said, "Good night" over my shoulder and slipped out.

As I passed the stairs, I heard Mrs. Ballinger coming up again, and she was muttering to herself. I laughed silently as I thought of Joe's enormous appetite, and I wondered if she was considering sending a bill to the township for his food after it was all over. That is, if it ever was all over. I got into Rhynda's room without her seeing me and found that Rhynda had fallen asleep with the light on and one hand still resting on her open book.

The wind was still high and blowing gustily around the house, and I shivered and started to undress quickly. I wanted to curl up in bed, with my head under the covers, and get warm. I tried to be quiet, in order not to disturb Rhynda, but she woke up just as I was putting on my dressing gown.

"Hullo," she said, yawning prettily. "I thought you were never coming. What on earth do you find to do around this moldy old tomb at all hours of the night?"

I glanced at the clock and saw that it was twenty minutes to one. I yawned myself, then. "God only knows," I said. "I don't."

She gave me an odd look from under her long curling lashes. "Maybe you've been trailing around after the boys."

"Well, yes," I said, "that does keep me pretty busy. There are several boys, and the trails are apt to cross and recross. It keeps me on the jump. Anyway, I'm going to the bathroom now. Maybe I'll meet one of them on the way. Be back in a minute." I walked out into the hall, leaving the door open as the bathroom light was off again.

I had got about halfway down the hall before it started, and then it began to drag its slow way across the attic floor. I stopped dead, my teeth biting into the back of my hand, as Rhynda's low wailing cry came from the bedroom behind me.

CHAPTER
22

SOMEHOW IT WAS NOT the dragging noise that horrified me so much this time; it was more Rhynda's desperate cry.

As I stood there uncertainly with my teeth knocking together, I heard Joe's feet thudding on the stairs. He passed me in the hall at a loping run and disappeared up the stairs to the attic. At the same time, a couple of bedroom doors were flung open, and I turned and went back into Rhynda's room.

She was lying with her head thrown back and her face pallid

while her body was trembling visibly. I did not know what to do for her, but I went over and pulled the bedclothes up around her neck and told her to be quiet, although she wasn't making any noise. It seemed like pretty feeble first aid, but at any rate she presently stopped shaking, and the greenish tinge disappeared from her face.

I arranged her pillow more comfortably, and after a moment she asked, "What are they doing out there?"

There were plenty of people in the hall by now. I could hear them milling around. I shrugged. "I don't know—nothing much, I guess. I think Joe must have made the attic just too late."

She moaned and moved her head from side to side. "Oh, God! It's Berg—"

"No," said Berg's voice from the doorway, "it isn't. And they're going to have to go some to get me. As a matter of fact, I hope they try, because then we'll know—"

"You'd better be careful, though," I said uneasily. "It's so easy to sneak up behind a person—"

"Don't worry," he said grimly. "I'm going to have eyes in the back of my head. But I came in to see if you were all right. Didn't one of you scream?"

"I did," Rhynda said faintly and pressed her hand against her head, as though it were aching.

"You mustn't worry, you'll be all right. I'm glad you're sleeping together here. Just lock the door and don't open it to anyone."

He went off, and Rhynda said scornfully, "How does he know it isn't one of us?"

"He recognizes the perfect lady when he sees her," I explained.

I started out for the bathroom again then. The hall was deserted, but I could hear Joe and several extra pairs of strong hands tearing the attic apart. There was a murmur of female voices in Mrs. Ballinger's room, but I passed it by quickly.

When I came out of the bathroom, I left the light on and the door open and went straight back to Rhynda's room. I locked the door and said, "There. Now if anyone tries to get in, we'll hear them, and if you happen to be 'they,' it's just my hard luck."

She laughed a little and pulled the bedclothes up around her neck as I opened the window. I got into bed with the firm intention of going straight to sleep, but the muffled thuds and bangings from the attic kept me alert in spite of myself. Rhynda seemed restless, too. I heard her turn twice, and after a while there was the snap and flare of a match as she lighted a cigarette.

"I might as well tell you," she said from the darkness, "that there isn't going to be any baby after all."

I raised my head sharply. "You mean you've had a miscarriage?"

"I guess so," she said cheerfully.

"But—but shouldn't you have a doctor, or something? How far on were you?"

She said gravely, "Nearly two weeks."

I lay back and laughed helplessly, and I heard her giggle with me.

"Talk about jumping to conclusions " I said, shaking my head.

"Well—but I was desperately afraid."

"I don't quite see why," I said slowly. "A baby isn't as bad as all that."

She was silent for a space, and then she said harshly, "Since I have to be a widow, I'm in a much better position if I'm free."

I was silent, and she must have sensed the fact that I found her a bit callous, for she said, "Don't you sneer, Leigh Smith. You're not married. Wait till your tin anniversary rolls around. You won't be so sentimental."

"Maybe not," I said, and let it go at that.

We fell silent, and I realized that the noises in the attic had stopped. The next minute I heard them all pour down into the hall, sounding like a herd of elephants, as men usually do when they're trying to be quiet.

I raised my head to listen and said eagerly, "I wonder if they found anything?"

"I don't know, and I don't care," Rhynda replied shortly. She had put out her cigarette, and she now settled down with her back to me, in a way that suggested that she did not want to talk any more.

Out in the hall they had started a discussion in piercing whispers and after I had listened to it for a few minutes, I couldn't stand it any more. I got up quietly, put on a dressing gown, and went to the door. Rhynda made no move, and I slipped out and closed it behind me.

Donald Tait, Richard, Berg, Joe and one of Joe's deputies were in a group not far from the door, and as the latch clicked they all turned and looked at me.

Joe sighed. "It's Nosey," he said resignedly. "I knew somebody was missin'."

They all laughed quietly, and I felt my face grow hot.

"Did you find it?" I asked. "The noise, I mean?"

"Yeah," said Joe.

"What is it? Tell me," I said eagerly.

"Suppose we put her to bed?" Richard suggested. "And make her wait until morning."

They all laughed again, and Joe said cheerfully, "Aw revoyer, Nosey."

"What's aw revoyer?" I asked coldly.

Joe explained kindly, "That's 'good-by' in French."

It reminded me of an old joke, so I said, "Oh. Well, guillotine."

"What?" said Joe suspiciously.

"That's good-by in French, too," I said, and found myself laughing alone. I swallowed it and turned back towards my door. "If you're going to hold out on me," I said furiously, "you can wait until the morning to hear what I was coming to tell you."

As I had hoped, five pairs of hands pulled me back, and they asked, practically in chorus, "What is it?"

"You'll tell me what I want to know first. I don't trust any one of you, and you can take it or leave it."

They took it, of course, and Richard and Berg did the explaining. They led me up to the attic and showed me that one of the wide floorboards had been ripped up all across the floor to the back of the house. A brick tied up in a piece of cloth lay on the plaster between the beams. It was tied around the middle with a piece of rope which ran along the plaster and out the end of the house through a hole that had been drilled especially for it.

After I had shaken my head over this contrivance, they took me downstairs again and along to the little sewing room that had the defective shutter. They pushed my head out the window, and I saw that the rope from the attic hung down behind the shutter and dangled some distance below it. An old flatiron was tied onto the end of it.

"You see," Richard explained, "it wasn't usually showing like this. The flatiron was tied on only when whoever arranged it wanted the brick to travel across the floor, and the wind had to be blowing or the thing wouldn't work. The weight of the iron alone was not sufficient to pull the brick, but when the wind blew it swung the iron a bit, and the brick moved along slowly. When the brick finally got all the way across and stopped at the wall, the iron was removed, and the brick returned to its starting point. When the brick is in its original place the rope doesn't hang down below the shutter and doesn't show."

"Was that floorboard loose in the attic?" I asked. Berg nodded. "Then why wasn't all this discovered before?"

Berg took me firmly by the arm and led me back to the hall. Donald Tait and the deputy had gone, but Joe still lounged against the wall, chewing his cud.

"She wants to know why all this was not discovered before," Berg said to him.

Joe sniffed. "Ask her about that bit of dirt she was gonna spill."

The three of them stood and looked at me expectantly, and my mind flew around like a squirrel in a cage. At last I said desperately, "Well, it's about the baby. I mean there isn't any."

"Is she feverish?" Richard asked, putting a hand on my forehead.

Joe said slowly, "You mean that baby whose father wasn't who he should've been?"

Berg murmured, "Rhynda?" and I said, "Well, er—"

Joe yawned. "Put Nosey to bed," he said. "I'm sleepy, but I can't settle down until she's outa the way."

Berg and Richard each took one of my arms and steered me back to Rhynda's room. They both gave me a kiss and put me firmly inside the door. I muttered, "Damn their casual kisses," and stubbed my toe.

The string of profanity that I let out relieved me and roused Rhynda. She said, "For God's sake, shut up!"

I climbed into bed and settled down and shortly fell into an uneasy sleep. I could not have slept more than half an hour when something aroused me. I glanced at the small illuminated clock by the bed and saw that it was a quarter to three. I could not hear any sound, but I knew that something had disturbed me, and I presently sat up and looked uneasily at Rhynda's bed.

It was empty.

CHAPTER
23

I LAY FOR A WHILE listening to the moaning of the wind and waiting for Rhynda to come back, presumably from the bathroom.

My thoughts trailed off rather drowsily to the idea that when I bought a house of my own, I'd make sure it was in a spot where there was no wind. I must have slept again briefly, for I roused suddenly, looked at the clock, and saw that it was ten minutes past three. Rhynda had been gone for twenty-five minutes!

I was wide awake now and thoroughly frightened. I knew that I'd have to go and search for her, and I was terrified of what I might find. I slipped out of bed, struggled into my dressing gown, and turned on the light. I satisfied myself that Rhynda was not in the room and then slowly opened the door into the hall.

It was pitch-dark out there and impossible to tell from where I stood whether the bathroom light was out or whether it was on and the door closed. I hesitated for a moment and then walked out into the hall, leaving the bedroom door wide open so that I would have as much light as possible.

I started down towards the bathroom and had not gone more than a few steps when a sound behind me caused me to look back sharply, just in time to see the door swing slowly to and shut with a faint click. I realized that it was probably the draft from the open window and reminded myself sternly that the doors in the house were well-built and usually closed quietly. But I was in a mild-panic, and I knew it. I was afraid to go back to the bedroom and afraid to go on, and I stood still in the darkness for a while with my teeth chattering.

I pulled myself together with an effort and decided to go on to the bathroom and see if Rhynda was there. I started down the hall again, but as my eyes grew more accustomed to the darkness, I became conscious of a grayish oblong which I recognized as the bathroom window. The door was open and the light off, then!

I stopped again, hesitating between going on and lighting the bathroom and going back to open the bedroom door. And as I stood there in the darkness and silence, I heard from downstairs, quite clearly and musically, the notes of the dinner gong!

I remained, frozen and fixed, while the thing played the chime that Doris always used to summon us to meals and went on to a faulty but recognizable attempt at "Swanee River." It had been John's favorite tune, I knew, and he had often sat at the piano and tried to pick it out with one finger, and even with one finger had made innumerable mistakes.

I whirled around and fled back to the bedroom, but with my hand on the knob my terror settled a little. Probably it was Rhynda walking in her sleep, or something of the sort. At any rate, someone ought to go down and bring her back to bed.

I swallowed a couple of times, squared my shoulders, and made for the stairs. I silently cursed Mrs. Ballinger for not having an up-stairs switch for the lower hall as I crept down through the darkness.

By the time I got to the bottom my fear had returned and I was in a cold sweat. Why had no one else heard the gong? And where was Joe? I realized, of course, that the notes of the gong were mellow rather than piercing, and that I probably would not have heard it myself if I had been in bed and asleep as I should have been.

I nearly retreated back up the stairs, but Rhynda was still on my mind, so I clung to the newel post and called her name in a quavering falsetto. There was no answering sound, and after a moment, I abandoned the newel post, made a dash across the hall, and switched on the light.

The gong was in the back part of the hall behind the stairs, and feeling better now that I was no longer walled in by darkness, I went around and had a look at it. It appeared to be as usual and was hanging still. I stared at it helplessly, and then my eyes traveled downwards to the floor beneath it, and I saw the gleam of a plain pin. I picked it up and knew somehow, even before I took it back to where the light was better, that it had a black head.

So now there was only one missing again. I stuck the one I had found in the collar of my dressing gown and wondered nervously if we'd ever find the other. I was distracted by a noise from the kitchen and I felt sure that it must be Rhynda. I made my way back there and cautiously opened the kitchen door.

The light was on, and Doris stood by the table. She was wrapped in a woolen bathrobe that was about two sizes too small, and her hair dangled down her back in a pigtail. I drew a little breath of relief and walked in.

She looked at me and said aggrievedly, "What in God's name is going on around here tonight?"

"I'd like to know myself. Did you hear the gong?"

She folded her arms. "I did, and I don't mind admitting that this dump gives me the creeps. I'm looking for another job, and when I find one, not even Joe is going to keep me here."

I sat down in a chair, rested my arms on the table, and gave a vast yawn. "I don't blame you. I'm going to get another job myself, one where you can sleep during the night. Have you heard anyone in the kitchen?"

She nodded. "About ten minutes ago, shortly before the gong went off. Say, listen, I'm going to make some coffee. Want some?"

"Why not? No use trying to sleep."

She busied herself noisily with the coffeepot and the cups and saucers, and I felt myself relaxing comfortably.

"Have you any idea who came in here?" I asked after a while.

She said, "Nope," and slid spoons into the saucers.

"Well, what did they do?"

"Tiptoed in, opened a drawer, fooled some with the things in the drawer, closed it and went out."

"Sounds like Joe," I said thoughtfully. "Do you know which drawer was opened, or whether anything was taken?"

"Nope, no notion. I never was much good at remembering what we're supposed to have, and unless they took something I use a lot, I don't guess I'll miss it, whatever it was."

I wanted her to look, then and there, to see if anything was missing, but she refused.

"What difference would it make," she said reasonably, "if I did find that something was gone? My land, child! You're getting to be as bad as Joe."

She brought the coffeepot to the table and sat down. I wanted to suggest that it might have been a knife that was taken, in which case we ought to rouse one of the men, but I felt sure she'd laugh at me, and anyway I was momentarily appalled at the idea that I might be getting as bad as Joe. I swallowed some scalding coffee and said instead, "But, Doris, who would ring that gong in the middle of the night? And why? It scares me, somehow. I'm afraid to go back to bed."

She chuckled. "Just you make a dash for it and don't stop to speak to any ghosts on the way. Serves you right for getting up in the first place. Once you go to bed in this Godforsaken place you should stay there until morning."

"I wish I had," I said dispiritedly.

She took a couple of gusty swallows and then suddenly put her cup down with a faint bang. "Say! Maybe it was the old lady ringing that gong. Maybe one of her attacks came on."

"Attacks?" I repeated, staring.

"Yeah. Mrs. Ballinger. Angina."

"Angina! But she couldn't. I'd have known about it."

"No, you wouldn't. She doesn't like anyone to know. She has a little thing hanging around her neck, some kind of medicine, and it has directions how to use it. I heard Rhynda and that Amy talking about it last summer. They were saying something about she hadn't had an attack for quite a while, and though they didn't come right out with it, they kinda talked like they expected the next one to finish her."

"But she should have told us! We might have wasted valuable time if she had had an attack when no one else was around."

"Maybe she's lying under the gong now," said Doris, with apparent unconcern.

I shook my head. "She's not there. I went there first. Unless she rang it and then went off somewhere."

"No," Doris said promptly. "Angina takes them quick. If she rang that gong for help, she'd be lying under it now."

We finished our coffee, and Doris stood up. "Well, don't you be scared, dearie. You just make a dash upstairs to your bedroom, and it'll all be over in a minute."

I thought of Rhynda and immediately convinced myself that she would be back in her bed by this time and that I had better take Doris's advice. She announced that she was going to leave the kitchen light on, said good night to me, and went off to her room.

I started into the back hall and then realized that the downstairs hall light had either gone out or been switched off. I backed into the kitchen again, relieved myself by swearing softly but luridly, and controlled a strong desire to cry.

I decided to go around by the butler's pantry, dining room, and the large drawing room, where I could turn on the lights as I went along. I got through the butler's pantry, and leaving the door wide, found my way easily to the dining-room switch. With the diningroom comfortably flooded with light, I started back to turn off the switch in the butler's pantry.

Something odd about the dining-room table caught my attention, and I turned to look. It was the telephone that I had last seen on the bedside table in my old room. I stared at it and then bent down to look at it more closely.

The mouthpiece was stained with blood.

CHAPTER
24

I TURNED AND RAN back to the kitchen with the intention of rousing Doris again, but with my hand raised to knock on her door, I hesitated. I'd feel a bit of a fool if it turned out that it was not blood on that telephone after all. Suppose, when I told Doris about it, she said, "Oh, I dropped that in some tomato ketchup."

"And how in hell," I whispered to myself, with my teeth chattering, "could Doris manage to drop an unused telephone into some tomato ketchup and then put it on the dining-room table without wiping it off?"

But standing alone in that empty, silent kitchen was worse than making a fool of myself to Doris, so I rapped smartly on her door. I heard her mutter, "Tch, tch," and then she plodded to the door and flung it open.

"Oh, Doris," I babbled, "there's an old telephone on the dining-room table, and there's blood on it."

She sighed and said patiently, "Listen, dearie, you're all excited, and I'm tired. Now you just run right upstairs, and get into bed, and you'll feel better in the morning."

"But the telephone! I tell you it has blood on it!"

"Tell Joe about it," she said firmly. "He's paid to listen to that stuff, and I have my own job. You go on up to bed. Good night."

The door closed with a click of finality, and I was left staring at its wooden surface and wondering at her nonchalant courage.

I turned away and thought miserably of the distance that separated me from my bed. I half considered screaming until someone came but discarded the idea almost immediately. I'd feel pretty silly when they all turned up, and all I could say was, "There's an old telephone in the dining room, and either it has blood on it or there's tomato ketchup around its mouth." I could imagine Richard grinning at me and knew he'd make some remark about the telephone being a sloppy eater.

I gave brief consideration to the idea of staying in the kitchen for the remainder of the night, but since it was almost as terrifying as going upstairs and would last longer, I decided against that too. There was nothing for it, then, but to go back to the bedroom, and I made up my mind to take Doris's advice and make a dash for it.

I did not wait to think any more about it, for fear I'd lose my courage. I ran through the back hall, around into the front hall, and made for the stairs. But halfway across the hall, I stopped dead. It was very dark, but not too dark to see that someone stood directly between me and the foot of the stairs.

I gasped, felt the sweat start on my forehead, and called in a voice I hardly recognized, "Is that you, Rhynda?"

There was no sound from the black shapeless thing, and at that moment Rhynda's voice floated down from the top of the stairs. "Leigh!" she said urgently. "Leigh Smith! Where in hell are you?"

I tried to answer and couldn't. I made some sort of strangled sound, and then the still figure moved and began silently to advance on me.

I turned and fled blindly, and after a moment I bumped heavily against a door. I wrenched it open, felt the sting of cold air on my face, and realized that I was on the front steps. A small portion of my mind registered thanks for the fact that since I had been off duty no one had bothered to lock the front door at night.

I flew down the steps and onto the path, which turned sharply, and ran along under the front windows. I wanted to get away from the house, but the path had a heavy border of shrubbery, and I was afraid that I would not be able to break through. So I kept to the path and almost immediately tripped over something and fell full length. It was something soft and bulky, and as I struggled desperately to get up, my hand touched a human face and came away wet and sticky.

I backed into the shrubbery and began to cry with horror and fear and cold. I knew that the inert body at my feet must have help and that I could not face the front hall again, alone. I clutched at the neck of my bathrobe with the numb fingers of the hand that was not sticky, and raising my head, shouted, "Help! Help! Help! Help!"

The first "Help" was a bit self-conscious, but the others were without inhibitions of any sort. I wanted someone to come.

I knew that Rhynda was awake, but her bedroom was on the other side of the house. I was standing directly under Amy's windows, and Donald Tait's room was on the corner. I shouted again, and after an interval Amy's room was lighted and she and Donald peered out.

"Get Joe!" I shrieked at them. "There's someone lying here hurt, and there's someone in the front hall, and I'm dying of cold!"

They disappeared, and shortly afterward lights were put on downstairs. I rushed back to the front door, then, and went in. Amy and Donald were in the hall, and Richard was just coming down the stairs.

"Couldn't find Joe," Donald said, and Amy added, "We got Richard."

I told them where to find the body, and the two men went out. I collapsed onto the bottom stair, and Amy leaned against the newel post and looked at me curiously. "What've you been crying for? What were you doing out there in the garden, at this time?"

"I lost a nickel there, this afternoon," I said shortly.

"Well, what are you mad about? Why can't you tell me what happened?"

"Wait till I get the rest of my audience," I said wearily. "I don't want to tell it ten times."

The sound of hurried footsteps upstairs was followed by Mrs. Ballinger's voice demanding shrilly, "What's going on down there?" I heard Rosalie Hannahs say immediately, "Now, my dear, you must be calm. We'll just go down and see." They started down together, and I reflected grimly that my place as companion seemed to be filled.

Richard and Donald were coming up the veranda steps, slowly and carefully, and Joe appeared suddenly, racing down the stairs and very nearly upsetting Rosalie and Mrs. Ballinger on the way.

"A trifle late, Joseph," I murmured, but he ignored me as he thudded past. He went to the assistance of Richard and Donald, and the three of them laid their burden on a couch in the drawing room.

It was Berg. He had a nasty wound in his forehead, and the blood had run down over his face. He was quite unconscious, and I thought he was dead. He had on pajamas, his dressing robe, and a pair of shoes.

Joe examined him briefly and announced that he was still alive, and I rushed to the telephone to summon Dr. O'Beirne. He answered himself and promised to come at once, and I went back to the drawing room. Joe gave me an evil look and asked what the blood was doing on my hand.

"Not a thing," I said, feeling a bit light-headed. "It has been waiting very patiently for me to wash it off."

The room and the people in it wavered a bit unsteadily before my eyes for a moment, and I heard myself saying distinctly, "The weapon will be found on the dining-room table, but you won't find my fingerprints on it, because I never touched it."

I could see Joe staring at me with narrowed eyes, and Richard said quickly, "Be quiet, Leigh. You're talking too much."

Joe departed for the dining room, and Rhynda came in. She went over to Berg and stood looking down at him and wringing her hands. She did not say anything. I reflected without venom that she had started me out on the night's series of horrors, and I wondered where she had been, but I did not like to ask her in front of the others.

Richard came to me and said in a low voice, "Why don't you stay in bed, Smithy, during the night? I'm afraid you're in for a spot of trouble now."

"The house can burn down around my head, before I'll do it again," I said bitterly. "But I wasn't the only one who was roaming around."

"Who else?" he asked quickly.

"Well, Rhynda, and somebody was standing at the foot of the stairs."

He shook his head. "That doesn't help much. Rhynda was with me, and if you couldn't recognize the other person, Joe probably won't believe in him."

My head drooped, and I stared at the floor in silence. So Rhynda had been with Richard in the small hours of the morning. I suddenly felt so desperately tired that I wanted to stretch out there on the drawing-room floor and sleep until Easter.

I looked at Berg's quiet figure and found my gaze concentrating on one of the limp hands. It lay palm upwards, with the fingers flexed, and a pin gleamed dully from one of the creases.

CHAPTER
25

JOE CAME BACK with the telephone. He had wrapped it in a soiled handkerchief, and I said hysterically, "Someone must have told you."

"Huh?"

"About fingerprints. Always wrap the weapon—"

Richard nudged me sharply and muttered, "Careful."

"What are you babblin' about?" Joe asked.

I gestured towards Berg. "There's a pin in his hand."

Joe and Richard leaned over the prostrate figure, and Joe carefully retrieved the pin. It had a black head, of course.

"Only one missin' now," Joe murmured thoughtfully.

I fumbled at the collar of my dressing gown and said, "No. Here it is."

Joe gave me a long hard stare. "I think it's about time you did a little explainin', and I want the whole story."

I gave it to him and was strongly of the opinion that he garnished it with a pinch of salt. He got Doris out of bed again, and she corroborated what she could. She seemed upset when she learned of Berg's condition and wanted to administer first aid, but the doctor arrived at that point, so she retired to the kitchen and put on a pot of coffee.

Dr. O'Beirne examined Berg briefly and observed that the wound was just above the temple, on the frontal bone. A fraction below and it would have been a good deal more serious. As it was, he would probably be all right, if he did not develop pneumonia. But he had lost a lot of blood, with a consequent lowering of his resistance, and pneumonia was possible, if not probable.

The doctor superintended his removal to his own bedroom upstairs, and Mrs. Ballinger led the procession, wringing her hands and getting in everybody's way. She took a seat by the sickbed and refused to be budged. The rest of us went down again for coffee.

Rosalie shook her head over it all until she must have been dizzy. "It's such a good thing you went down, Leigh. You see, the doctor says if he had been left to lie out there all night he would almost certainly have died by morning."

"I can't understand why the gong was played," I said thoughtfully. "Surely interference of any kind was the last thing that was wanted."

"Maybe it was the wind," Rosalie suggested brightly.

"The wind," I said patiently, "probably would not know how to play 'Swanee River.'"

Joe set his cup down and dried his mouth with the back of his hand. He looked at me with a gimlet eye and asked ominously, "Who, besides you, heard that gong ring, anyways?"

I looked guilty at once, as I always do when I am perfectly innocent, and while I was trying desperately to remember whether Doris had mentioned hearing it, Donald Tait spoke up unexpectedly.

"I did," he said. "I heard it distinctly, and then I heard someone go downstairs."

Joe flicked him a glance and asked, "Anybody else?"

Donald said, "Yes. Amy."

Amy's eyes flashed angrily. "I did not hear it," she said hotly. "I never heard a thing!"

Rhynda gave a slow, aggravating laugh. "It's all right, Amy. Dear Aunt Mabel is upstairs and out of earshot." She raised her long lashes and fixed Rosalie Hannahs with a cool, lazy stare. "You may have to fix Rosalie, of course," she added deliberately.

"Rhynda Ballinger, I don't know what you're talking about!" Rosalie protested, on the verge of tears. Joe waved them to silence and concentrated on Amy. "Did you or did you not hear that gong?"

"Well, only very faintly," she said, glaring at him defiantly.

"I don't believe she hears as well as Donald," Rhynda said sweetly and flashed a warm smile at Mr. Tait, who smiled back. I looked with fear and trembling at Amy, but apparently she had not noticed, because she failed to explode.

Richard and Joe had disappeared quietly after Amy's admission, and my mind had followed them restlessly. I found that I could not sit still, and after a while, I got up and wandered out into the hall. They were both there, carefully examining the floor.

Joe was on his hands and knees in front of the door to what we called the reception room. It was a small room at the front of the house that was never used. Richard was at the edge of the rug that lay in the exact center of the hall. As I walked out, he said, "Nothing here."

"Well, here's one," Joe announced with subdued triumph.

Richard straightened up hastily, and I followed him. Joe was pointing to a small drop of blood on the floor in front of the door to the reception room. Richard opened the door, and we went in and switched on the light. The single window was wide open, and on the floor beneath it was another drop of blood.

They both looked out of the window, and I squeezed my head

between them and looked out, too. The spot where Berg had been found was directly below us. Between the path and the house there was a narrow flowerbed, and although the earth was, of course, pretty hard, we could see in the light from the window that there were two fresh indentations in it. They looked like heelmarks.

"Looks like he was hit at the door, carried to the window, and thrown out," Joe observed sagely.

But Richard shook his head. "Berg is a big man, and it would not be easy to carry him from the door to the window, and harder still to lift him and throw him out. And granted that it could have been done, there would have been a lot more blood spilled. I think he was hit at the window and pushed out as he fell. Whoever hit him probably aimed for the temple, but got it a bit too far up. It was well thought out, because if the blow did not kill him, the exposure almost certainly would. Smithy's nocturnal rambling could hardly have been foreseen, of course.

"It was the same in Freda's case. She was drowned after the blow. Whoever is doing it tries to make doubly sure. I think there's no doubt that Berg owes his life to the person who played that gong."

"I intend to find out about that," Joe said. "But this guy ain't so smart. He don't kill them off at the first smack. If the Freda dame had been found sooner, she coulda been pulled around all right."

"Well, she'd have to have been discovered almost at once," Richard said doubtfully. "At that, she had a much better chance of being found than Berg did."

Joe moved restlessly. "But look," he said presently, "with your theory, how do you account for the blood over by the door?"

"I suppose it fell from the telephone as it was being taken to the dining room."

"But why take it to the dining room?" I asked reasonably.

Joe groaned, "Jeez! It'll be good to be done with this case. And the best thing about it will be not havin' you tailin' me around twenty-four hours out of each day."

He went off, pulling a flashlight out of his pocket and saying he was going to study the possible heelmarks in the flower bed.

"Woman's place is in the home, Smithy," Richard murmured reprovingly.

"I've had enough home to last me the rest of my life," I said gloomily. "I'm going to live in the park and eat nuts."

He smiled at me and rumpled my hair around. "How about a nice steam-heated apartment with all the rooms on one floor, and only four or five at that?"

I was thinking about Rhynda having been in his room, so I moved my head away and shrugged.

He said suddenly, "I have an idea. Where's that little book with the list of things you found in the various bedrooms?"

"It's upstairs. Why?"

"You go and get it," he said earnestly. "Take it to my room, and wait there for me. I'll come up as soon as I can get away from Joe. I don't want to confide in Joe just yet. He might do things I wouldn't like."

"How long do you expect to keep me waiting?" I asked doubtfully.

"Not long, I promise."

He dashed off after Joe, and I went slowly upstairs. I felt a bit annoyed with him. If he thought he was some sort of a lady-killer, entertaining all the girls in his room, then I declined to be among those present.

I got the little book from under my pillow, went to Richard's room, and pinned a note on his pillow to the effect that I would wait for him in my own old room. I went there forthwith, the little shopping list still clutched firmly in my hand. I sat down and began silently to curse Richard, the lady-killer. I admitted to myself that I was one lady he had killed, but no one, I said to myself firmly, would ever know it, unless he became really serious. I was musing on this possibility, despite his obvious friendliness with Rhynda, when the door opened and Rhynda herself walked in.

"I read your note," she said, stretching herself out on the bed, "but let me give you a little word of warning. Don't get serious over one Richard Jones, because he and I are going to be married quite soon."

CHAPTER
26

I SAID PROMPTLY, "Congratulations."

She looked at me from under the arm she had thrown across her forehead. "Why?" she asked. "Or is it Berg you were after?"

"May I have Berg, then?" I said politely.

She pulled herself off the bed abruptly and said, "Oh, shut up!" and started for the door.

"Are you mad," I asked, "because I didn't pull down my hair and cry?"

She turned around and said slowly, "As a matter of fact, I am—but I suppose I'll get over it. In the meantime, I'll console myself with the sure knowledge that you won't get Berg, either."

She went out and banged the door, and I sat there, wondering what had made her angry. Rhynda was never mean unless she was angry.

I didn't think much about Richard—I didn't want to—but I was conscious of a faint relief that I had never showed him I was serious, and I earnestly vowed that I never would. Having settled that with myself, I began to wonder why he had not turned up and realized suddenly that Rhynda had probably destroyed my note.

I went out into the hall and passed Rosalie Hannahs, who was bustling along in the direction of Berg's room. "Patient's easier now," she called cheerfully. "Mabel and I are taking good care of him."

"Mabel!" I thought scornfully. "What does Rosalie expect to get out of all this? Berg, maybe, since I can't have him?"

I giggled to myself as I thought of Berg standing up at the altar beside Rosalie in the sort of wedding clothes she'd be sure to pick out for herself. I remembered the odd thing I had found in Rosalie's room when I had searched the bedroom—a train ticket to Elkton, Maryland, the eloper's Mecca, but it had never been used.

I knocked on Richard's door and he answered at once.

"No wonder you were fired out of your job," he said aggrievedly. "You never do what you're told. I've been waiting here for half an hour."

"Now that we are no longer engaged," I said with dignity, "you can't bawl me out like that. Nor can you tell me where to get off at, or to head in, and I won't accept either cards or spades from you."

He laughed and pulled me into the room. "When did you break the engagement?" he asked chattily.

"About ten minutes ago. Rhynda and I tossed for you, and she lost."

He laughed again. "Rhynda can breathe easily. She has red hair, and an old aunt of mine once told me that a person of my coloring should never marry a redheaded woman. Besides, you can't stand me up like that. I told the family the wedding was February 15 and the bride a blonde. Everything will be arranged by now, and my dear old aunt will have ordered the decorations in pale pink and baby blue."

"I don't want to upset everything," I said reasonably, "but you'd better make it the sixteenth. My aunt Hortense's birthday is on the fifteenth, and if I don't go around there with all the other sucker relations, she might leave me out of her will."

"The sixteenth," he said gravely, and jotted it down in a notebook. Then he kissed me as though he meant it, but I was too busy being afraid that Rhynda might walk in to enjoy it much.

He became businesslike after that, and took the shopping list from me. We sat down on a settee that had been covered with chintz from the five-and-dime, a rather unique pattern which was made up of sprays of lilac and nasturtium growing out of the same red flowerpot.

"It's a pity to sit on the flowers," I murmured, but he ignored me and fixed his attention on the little book.

He pored over it for some time to himself. Once he asked abruptly, "Where did that old telephone come from?"

"Mrs. Ballinger's clothes closet—always kept there. Also it was in my old room, on the bedside table, earlier this evening."

"How do you know?"

"I saw it," I said, "and raised my eyebrows at it."

"Well, don't tell Joe anything about it—he'll run you in. He's determined to run somebody in before lunch so that he can snap his fingers at the interfering louses."

I gave an involuntary shiver and Richard returned to the notebook. He was silent for so long this time that I began to get bored. I patted my hair, scuffled my feet around, and at last said conversationally, "Did you ever hear about Mrs. Ballinger's angina ? "

He looked up quickly. "What was that?"

"Mrs. Ballinger's angina pectoris. Rumor has it that she will probably go off in her next attack, but she hasn't had one for a long time."

I was utterly unprepared for his reaction to this piece of gossip. He sprang up and almost shouted, "But why didn't you tell me? Why on earth didn't you tell me?"

"I didn't know it myself until the early hours of this morning," I said defensively.

He began to pace the room agitatedly, his head slightly bent. I watched him until he stopped and stared down at me, his eyes somber.

"I think I've got it, Leigh. It seems rather ghastly and unbelievable, but it can't be any other way. I don't see how I can be wrong." He took two more turns about the room and stopped in front of me again. "Listen, Smithy, I'll run over the clues and then with what you know perhaps you'll see it the way I do."

I began to be infected by his excitement. "Go ahead," I said eagerly.

"First, I'll read over this list of things you found in the various bedrooms. Rosalie's: unused train ticket to Elkton, Maryland, dated several years ago. Rhynda: unpaid bill from a trainer for training a Russian wolfhound for show."

"Rhynda doesn't like dogs," I pointed out.

"A Russian wolfhound is not, rightly speaking, a dog," said Richard. "It's a decoration, and Rhynda is nothing if not decorative. But, to go on, Mrs. Ballinger: a solicited prospectus for a boys' school. Richard Jones: a set of false teeth. I'll explain that."

"I'm all ears," I said politely.

"They belong to my father and some day they will be mine."

"They're not yours yet," I said, "and in the meantime, don't you think he'll be wanting them?"

"No. He uses them only when his Sunday set gets out of order. These were to have been dropped at the dentist's to have a missing tooth replaced, but I forgot them and found them still in my pocket when I arrived here."

"All right. Get on with it."

"Berg: a list of words on a piece of paper—'The Elms, Far Point, Windy Point, Harrington.'"

"Harrington is Berg's middle name," I observed.

"Quite right, and stop interrupting. Amy: a maternity dress, size twenty. Am I right in concluding that even if Amy were going to have a baby, any gown in size twenty would be too large for her?"

"You are 'quate rate,'" I said primly.

"All right. Next, Donald Tait: a box of stink bombs. What are stink bombs, Smithy?"

I looked at him in astonishment. "No imagination," I concluded, "and certainly not the right kind of schooling. They are bombs that stink but don't kill. Routine school child's equipment, at least in my day."

"Hmm. Possibly a practical joker. By the way, wasn't there anything odd in your room?"

I blushed and said defiantly, "A set of the Elsie Dinsmore books. I found them in the attic, and I've had the *best* time with them. The way the poor little dear suffers—"

"I won't tell on you," he said, grinning. He sat down and was silent for a while, then he said, "You've just heard that list—add to it the telephone as a weapon—one drop of blood beside the door, and another at the window—the heelmarks in the flower bed—the gong playing—Amy and Donald looking out of the same window—Mrs. Ballinger's sudden friendship with Rosalie Hannahs, who is living in her house and eating her food without paying for either—and last, but far from least—Mrs. Ballinger's angina. What do you make of it?"

"Nothing," I said promptly. "At that, you've left out a couple of things. Doris heard someone moving around in the kitchen, apparently looking for something, before the gong was played. And Rhynda being in your room for three quarters of an hour or longer."

"I can't place the kitchen episode," he said, "unless it was Joe, or one of his boyfriends, but perhaps it isn't important. As for Rhynda, she was in my room for perhaps five minutes, certainly not longer."

"Then where was she the rest of the time?"

He was unexpectedly interested in this, and I had to tell him exactly when I had first looked at the clock after I had discovered that Rhynda was gone, at what time I had left the room, and about how long I had stayed downstairs.

He considered it and said slowly, "Then Rhynda could have played that gong. When she came in to me, she said she was frightened, that she had been to the bathroom and had lost her nerve in the dark hall on her way back. I turned on the light and talked to her for a bit, and then I opened my door so that the light would shine out into the hall and escorted her back to her room. I went straight back to bed and to sleep, and woke up again when hell started to pop."

"When she came back to her room I was missing," I said thoughtfully, "so I suppose she came out again, and that's when she called over the banister to me. Probably she heard some noise downstairs.

Anyway, there seems to be about twenty minutes of her time that wants accounting for."

"She could have been in the bathroom for twenty minutes before you came out, and in my room when you went downstairs."

"It sounds like the four Marx brothers," I said doubtfully.

We were silent for a while, and then I asked him about the black-headed pins. "You forgot to put them in your list of clues, didn't you?"

"No, I didn't forget them, but I don't know how to explain them." He stood up. "I think I have the rest, though. I'm pretty sure I know who is responsible for all this. I'm going to find Joe now, but I want you to sit there and think it all over, I want to know if you come to the same conclusion that I did."

He left the room and I raised my stiff body from the flowerpots and went and lay down on the bed. "Maybe I can make Joe jealous," I thought and giggled sleepily. At the end of five minutes, I was nearly asleep, and then the door opened suddenly and Rhynda walked in.

She looked at me venomously—and she held in her hand a small, bright kitchen knife.

CHAPTER
27

I STARTED UP NERVOUSLY and exclaimed, "My God, Rhynda! What are you doing with that knife?"

"What are you doing in here?" she countered angrily. "Damn it, didn't I warn you away from Richard? Are you trying to make a fool of yourself?"

"I don't have to try," I said, with my eyes on the knife. "I was born to it. But I'm not going to fight with you over Richard. To hell with him, you can have him on a plate, and I'll stick parsley in his ears. I wouldn't want a man who can't make his own choice."

She said, "Damn you," softly and almost fretfully, and glanced absentmindedly at the knife in her hand. Then she widened her eyes and looked straight at me. "He has made his choice, and it's I. He made it some months ago."

I remembered the brief expression of black anger on John's face when Rhynda had been carrying on with Richard on Christmas Eve, and after a moment I said slowly, "Are you trying to tell me—"

"You know very well what I'm telling you. That pig, Rosalie, meant what she said at the seance, only I don't know how she found out about it."

Suddenly I didn't want to pursue it any further. I asked impersonally, "What are you doing with the knife?"

She seemed to relax. "I was cold downstairs, so I put on my tweed jacket—it was hanging in the hall closet down there. I put my hands in the pockets and found this thing."

"What are you going to do with it?"

She shrugged. "I don't know. Throw it out of the window, I guess."

"Give it to me," I said, "and go on back to bed."

She handed it over, and I walked with her to her room and helped her into bed. As she stretched out, she seemed suddenly to lose all her vitality, and she looked deathly tired. She made no further sound or movement, but I knew that she was crying quietly.

It was half past five, and after a moment's thought I threw off my bathrobe and dressed quickly. When I had finished, I switched off the light and left the room.

Mrs. Ballinger and Rosalie were still on duty in Berg's room. The door was half open, and I could hear them talking together in low tones. I lingered outside for a while and did a bit of eavesdropping, but they were merely discussing ways and means of cutting down the expense of the table without actually resorting to bread and water. I passed on quietly and heard Amy and Donald talking in Amy's room. I felt no inclination to listen in there so continued on downstairs.

Doris had gone back to bed and Richard seemed to be engaged in a thorough search of the entire lower floor. Joe and two of his deputies were outside. Dr. O'Beirne had gone.

"What are you looking for?" I asked Richard.

"Haven't you been able to figure it out?"

I shook my bead and showed him the knife. "This isn't what you're looking for, is it?"

He examined it carefully, while I told him about it, and said at last, "It's not what I'm after, but it makes me more sure than ever that the thing I want is around here, somewhere."

"Can't you tell me what it is?" I asked impatiently.

"Please, Leigh, sit down somewhere and put your head to work. I want you to come to the same conclusion as mine, but I want you to come to it independently. Then I'll know that we must be right."

I curled up in an arm chair and fished out a cigarette, and after fifteen minutes of quiet, I realized disgustedly that I had used the time to consider whether or not Rhynda's inferences about herself and Richard had any foundation in fact. I tried to forget it and to concentrate on Richard's list of clues, but my mind returned obstinately to Richard and to an unhappy conviction that she was telling the truth. I realized that I was getting nowhere, and shrugging the thing away from me impatiently, I stood up abruptly.

It was getting light by now, and I went to the hall and got a coat from the closet. I slipped out the front door and went down the path to the spot where I had found Berg. I stared indifferently at the frozen ground and spared a glance at the two semicircular heelmarks in the garden bed, where he must have landed. On the path, where his head had been, there were two drops of blood.

I sighed, hunched my coat around my neck, and started gloomily back to the house. I had gone perhaps three steps when a shaft of brilliant light seemed to strike into my consciousness. I flew up the porch steps and through the door and began a casual search in the small music room.

After a minute or two, a voice said behind me, "No use looking here—I went through it thoroughly a little while ago."

I turned and faced Richard, my eyes wide and strained.

"Joe's been through here, too," he added.

I sat down. "Then the best thing to do is to sit and think out where it is."

"Right."

He sat down near me and offered me a cigarette. After a while I said, "I don't know why the black-headed pins puzzle you. I think they mean the same thing as the telephone being used as a weapon."

"I did think of that," he admitted. "But you remember the one you found outside, where John had fallen? You found it a day or so later, and yet it was quite bright and shiny, so that I think it had not been there until the day you found it."

I said, "Yes, but I believe the one found in the bathroom closet was not an accident."

He nodded. "Right you are. But come on, Smithy, we've wallowed in it long enough, for the time being. Let's get some breakfast. I'll make you a pfannkuchen."

I said, "Well, er—bacon and eggs are always nice."

"So are my pfannkuchens," he replied with dignity.

I resigned myself. "All right. I suppose you've been dying to make one. I'll be the victim."

"You won't regret it."

"I doubt it," I said gloomily and went on upstairs, because I'd forgotten to put on any lipstick.

I looked in on Berg and found Mrs. Ballinger and Rosalie busily engaged in changing the dressing on his head. The wound was exposed—an ugly gash, straight and very long—and I shuddered and backed out hastily. Mrs. Ballinger hissed after me that I need not come in again. I was not wanted.

By the time I got downstairs again, it occurred to me to wonder why they were changing the dressing on the wound so soon after the doctor had attended to it. It seemed to me, too, that Mrs. Ballinger had veered around a bit. A short time ago she had been proposing Berg to me as a possible future husband and now she was practically throwing me out of his sickroom.

In the kitchen, Richard was busy with a frying pan which contained something that looked like a bit of old mattress. When I appeared, he halved it and scooped it out into two plates.

"Coffee's nearly ready," he said cheerfully.

"Then put those bits of rubber tire in the oven until it is ready. A good cook always brings everything to a finish at once. Anyway, we'll need the coffee to wash that muck down with."

"You'll eat those words, Smithy, after you've tasted it."

"It'll be easier than eating the pfannkuchen," I said. "Listen, why do you suppose Mrs. Ballinger and Rosalie Hannahs are changing Berg's dressing already when the doctor fixed him up only a little while ago?"

He had just put the two plates in the oven, and he turned around and looked at me in astonishment. "They're changing Berg's bandage?"

I nodded. "I walked in on them while they were doing it."

"Take care of the coffee," he said. "I'm going up."

He went off in a hurry, and a moment after Joe lounged in. He glanced at the table, yawned, and said, "Eatin' again?"

I didn't bother to answer. I redivided the pfannkuchen into three and got out another cup and saucer. Joe sat down at the table and began absentmindedly to pick his teeth.

"Wait till after the pfannkuchen," I said. "You'll get much better results."

He ignored me, and after a while Richard came back. I poured the coffee, and we sat down.

"What did they say?" I asked, glancing at Richard.

"They said the doctor had done a punk job, and Rosalie claimed she knew how to do it better. I threw out my chest and gave them hell."

"What did they do?"

"Threw me out," he said equably. "I believe one of them even heaved a magazine after me."

"What's all this?" Joe asked, with his mouth full.

Richard started to explain, and while he was in the middle of it, an idea came to me.

"Hey!" I shouted. "I've thought of another place to look. I don't know why it would be there, but it just might."

"It's a rank excuse to leave your pfannkuchen," Richard said coldly.

"You said it!" I murmured. "Joe, lend me a toothpick, will you?"

Joe passed one over, and I said hastily, "Never mind—it's out."

I led them to the front door, and they followed me out and down the path. I went on to where the shrubbery ended at the driveway, circled around, and came back to the spot where Berg had been found, only now we were on the other side of the shrubbery, and it was so thick that we could not see through.

It was there, a white cloth runner from a side table in the dining room, caught on the heavy leaves of a rhododendron bush and soaked with blood.

CHAPTER
28

RICHARD SAID, "The missing blood. And we find it on a cloth."

Joe picked the cloth up gingerly, and we all started slowly back to the house. As we neared the front door, he said suddenly, "That gong—who in hell rang it?"

"Berg, of course," Richard replied promptly. "He wanted to attract someone's attention."

Joe frowned. "I thought we decided it happened right by the

window, nowheres near the gong."

Richard murmured, "I doubt it," and I broke in with a point of my own.

"Anybody who could move John's body from the bed to a chair and carry Freda's body from her room to mine could also drag Berg along to the window and topple him out."

"Yeah, but why didn't he yell, instead of playin' the gong?" Joe objected.

Before we could reply, he went on heavily. "Unless it happened like this. He was smacked near the gong and was layin' on the floor under it. He was nearly out, but he seen the thing reachin' almost to the floor, the way it does, with the stick hangin' at the side, low down. So he banged on it, but the noise brought the murderer back in a hurry, and he was dragged to the front room and thrown out the window for his pains."

"Would there have been time for all that?" Richard asked me.

"I think so," I said doubtfully. "But when you're scared and don't know what to do next, you lose all sense of time."

We were standing in the front hall by this time, and Joe suddenly lost interest in us. "Well, I'm goin' off to wind this thing up," he said briskly and disappeared up the stairs, two at a time.

"Don't get caught in the coils," I trilled and got no answer.

"He's always finding you messing around in the coils when he tries to wind up," Richard said severely.

"Don't you worry about Joe and me," I replied airily. "We understand each other. And someday, we're going out together and really eat."

"Not if Joe sees you first. I'm willing to bet you won't see his heels for dust when this case is over. But stop the idle chatter, Smithy. We have work to do. And the first thing on the list is a cozy little get-together with Rhynda."

"Rhynda?" I repeated coldly.

"She knows something—or everything. She's behaving oddly. Hasn't she suggested to you that she and I were something more than acquaintances?"

I laughed shortly. "There was no suggestion about it. She damn well told me."

"Flagrant falsehood," he declared earnestly.

"What kind?" I asked interestedly.

"Listen, Smithy. I met Rhynda exactly twice before the Christmas Eve binge, and both times she was accompanied by John and I was in the company of Berg. I'm not quite clear about it, but I believe we had the weather up for discussion and went into every angle of it."

I was vaguely conscious that, quite against my will, my face had wreathed itself in smiles, and I murmured inadequately, "Is that so?"

He stared at me for a moment of silence, and then he asked abruptly, "Were you thinking of your lunch when your face lit up like that?"

"No," I said, scowling heavily, "I just found a nickel in my pocket."

"If you'll stop fooling around for five minutes, perhaps we can get somewhere. About Rhynda. She has no need to chase after men, and I don't think she cares particularly for me, so that the whole thing needs explaining. Come on, we'll go and find her."

I trotted after him, but I was firmly convinced that if he thought he could get Rhynda's story merely by asking for it, he was sadly mistaken. We looked upstairs first, but Rhynda was not there, and we finally tracked her down in the dining room, having breakfast with Amy and Donald Tait.

Richard jerked out two chairs, seated me and then himself, and poured two cups of coffee. He handed me one, and I looked at it with loathing. It seemed to me that I had been drinking coffee pretty steadily since dinner the night before. Richard glanced a me and muttered out of the corner of his mouth, "Drink it up, damn you."

Rhynda gave us a long lazy stare and then flicked her eyes at Donald Tait for an instant. "If either of you men ever wants to come unstuck from the woman who is always hanging around your neck, do come to me for advice. I'm sure I can show you a way out of your difficulty."

Amy started to shout immediately but had not got any farther than, "What do you mean, Rhynda Ballinger—" when Donald nudged her and whispered something to her that shut her up. She subsided into sullen, angry silence.

"I don't mind sharing," I said brightly. "If Amy is willing, we can split the two of them three ways."

Amy spat some inaudible remarks into Donald's ear, and Rhynda said in a bored voice, "Sporting of you."

I added pleasantly, "Either one of you can have Mr. Jones on his cooking days, all day. And you won't have to cook a thing. In fact, I insist upon it."

"You snake," Richard murmured.

Amy pushed her chair back from the table and stood up. Donald got up more slowly, and she took a firm hold on his arm. "You silly fools!" she said, and marched him out of the room.

Rhynda smiled faintly and turned to me. "You don't want that coffee, Leigh, you make a face every time you sip at it. Suppose you vanish and let me talk to Richard for a while, whether it's one of his cooking days or not."

"Why, certainly," I said promptly.

I got up, went out of the door, and closed it carefully behind me. Then I walked straight to the kitchen and on to the butler's pantry. The swinging door that opened into the dining room was closed, and I murmured, "The honor of the Smiths ," and laid my ear to the crack.

Doris called after me, "Did you take my vegetable knife? I can't find it high or low, and there's never two of anything in this place."

I glanced back at her and put my finger to my lips, and she dropped her voice to a subdued grumbling. I put my ear back in place.

"But, Rhynda," Richard was saying, "you must have had a reason for trying to queer me with Leigh."

"Well, of course," she said lightly. "Naturally I had a reason."

"What was it?"

"Oh, I simply took a fancy to you. And you can't deny that you showed me some attention on Christmas Eve."

"I can't swallow that. You're not the sort to reach out after a man whose interest is obviously somewhere else. Aside from anything else, you don't have to. You can attract hordes of men without the slightest effort. Besides, you went to some lengths. Do you mind telling me just how far you did go?"

There was a short silence, and then Rhynda said, "Why? Didn't she tell you?"

"No, but you couldn't miss it. I knew immediately. It's quite clear that I'm in bad. Be a sport, Rhynda, and clear me."

I heard her giggle, and she said in a high, prim voice, "All the statements that I made about Richard Jones and myself are false."

"Say it a bit louder," he urged, "so that Leigh can hear."

I felt my face grow hot, and Rhynda said sharply, "What do you mean?"

Richard called amiably, "Why don't you come in here, Nosey, and be comfortable."

I went in then, resumed my chair, and took out a cigarette in an effort to be nonchalant.

Rhynda's eyes flashed, and she turned on Richard angrily. "Did you deliberately place her outside that door to listen?"

"Of course not. But I knew she'd be listening in somewhere. The Smith blood will tell."

"All I heard was the last of it," I said to Rhynda pacifically.

"Let's get back to business," Richard said urgently. "I think I'm beginning to see why you tried to pretend that we were secret lovers, Rhynda."

Her face colored darkly, and she sprang up from her chair and stood staring at him. He went on quietly, "You know all about these murders, don't you? You know who is responsible, and why. And you're frightened. You're trying to cover up by pretending that you're something more than an intimate friend of mine."

She cried desperately, "You're a hateful liar!" and flew out of the room.

Richard and I looked at each other. "Must have hit home," he said thoughtfully.

I nodded and looked up as Joe walked in.

"What's eatin' that Jane?" he asked irritably, jerking a thumb over his shoulder. "She comes steamin' up the hall, smacks into me, and then swears at me."

"What did she say?" I asked.

But Joe had something else on his mind. "I just checked on them black-headed pins," he said, "and there's another one missing from the old lady's collection."

CHAPTER
29

RICHARD STOOD UP. "We'll go and look for it, here and now. You have all the others—all the exhibits?"

"Just looked 'em over," said Joe. "All O.K., includin' the ones in Skinny here's room."

Richard nodded. "All right. We'll find the one that's missing if we have to tear the place apart. We'll start upstairs—more likely to be up there, I think."

"Right," agreed Joe, and they made for the stairs, while I followed closely behind.

They paused in the upper hall, and I pulled up behind them.

"How shall we manage it," Richard asked, "without anyone knowing about it?" I pushed my head in between them. "You want to keep it a secret?"

"From everyone but you," Richard admitted. "We wouldn't attempt the impossible."

"Now wait," said Joe. "I got it. Seein' as we can't get rid of Nosey here, and seein' also as she searches like she was trained to it, and nobody knows it better than me, I'll take her into the bedrooms with me to hunt, and you stay outside and watch. If anyone comes along, you tell them to go on down to the parlor and wait, because I want to question them."

"You're the boss," Richard said aggrievedly, "but don't think you're pulling the wool over my eyes. And you shouldn't mix business with pleasure. If you want a chance to be alone with her—"

"Cut it out!" Joe exploded. "If I want to get fancy on the side, I can always do better than a bag of bones."

We started with Rosalie's room and went through it thoroughly, without result. From there, we went on to Rhynda's room, where we were occupied for a considerable time, and I could hear Richard moving about impatiently outside the door.

Amy's room came next, and it was there that I found the pin, stuck in a fold of the window curtain.

Joe had run a sharp eye over my dress before we started to make sure that the pin was not already sticking in it, and he had watched me like a hawk while I was searching to prevent what he called funny business. So when I pulled the pin from the curtain and called, "Here it is," he felt reasonably certain that I had not brought it along and put it there in the first place.

He was jubilant. "Jeez! I never woulda thought of the curtain. I knew what I was doin' when I brought you along to snoop."

Richard opened the door and came in. "Found it?"

Joe showed it to him. "I'm all set now—I'm gonna make an arrest."

"Have you all the proof you need?"

"Sure," said Joe confidently. "But I'll get a confession out of them."

"You mean there are two of them?" I asked, staring.

"Yep," said Joe briefly.

"I think we ought to question Berg first," Richard suggested. "We haven't asked him if he remembers anything of what happened to him last night. The doctor has just left him again, and he says we may question him, as he seems to be all right."

"O.K. No harm in that. Did you send anyone down to the parlor, to be questioned?"

"Rhynda, Amy and Donald," Richard said, and Joe nodded.

We went along to Berg's room, knocked at the door, and walked in. Rosalie and Mrs. Ballinger were there, and Mrs. Ballinger sprang up from her chair and came towards us excitedly.

"You can't come in here—you'll have to go out. Berg is in a serious condition, and I won't have him disturbed."

Richard said soothingly, "We don't want to disturb him, Mrs. Ballinger, but the doctor just told me that he was quite all right, and that we might question him."

Mrs. Ballinger's face became mottled with red, and her voice sprang from a higher note. "I don't care. This is my house, and I tell you you are not to bother him."

"It's all right, Aunt Mabel," Berg said from the bed. "I'm feeling quite well enough to talk."

He was wearing a gaily striped dressing gown and was sitting propped up with pillows and smoking a cigarette. His aunt fell back a few steps and looked at him uncertainly.

"I must tell them what I can," he said to her, gently, "and any delay makes it harder for them."

"Thanks, Berg," said Richard. "Begin at the beginning, will you?"

But Berg started off with a question. "Who found me?" he asked, looking around at us.

Joe and I spoke together. I said, "I did," and Joe said, "Nosey, of course, guaranteed to find anything."

Berg looked at me and said, "Thanks, Leigh. Seems that you saved my life. But how did you come to find me?"

"Now listen," Joe broke in, "we've heard her story plenty already, and we wanta hear yours."

Rosalie said, "Please, gentlemen, come to the point, and let's have it over with. My patient should be perfectly quiet."

I looked at her and realized that she was enjoying herself immensely. "Nothing like tending the sick for keeping some women amused," I thought pensively.

Berg laughed shortly. "Won't take me long to come to the point. Something woke me up last night, and I sat up on my elbow and distinctly heard someone going down the back stairs—the stairs, by the way, are right next to this room. I thought at first it was Joe or one of his henchmen, but then it struck me that whoever it was was being too quiet—there was too much —well—stealth. Joe and Company always clatter wherever they go, possibly because they buy their shoes at the same place." He paused and looked at Joe. "Cholmondedly's, in New York, is a good place for shoes, old man."

"If it's the same place," said Joe equably, "that you got them lavender underpants I seen you wearin', I ain't havin' any truck with it."

Berg grinned at him and went on. "I was uneasy about it, and at last I got up, put on my dressing gown, and went downstairs. I found my way to the kitchen, put on the light there, and walked through into the dining room."

"Did you open a drawer in the kitchen and get something out?" Joe interrupted.

"No," Berg said. "I went through the dining room and on into the drawing room, turning on and off the lights on my way. I got to the front hall and turned on the light there, then I went a little way down into the back hall, and the light went out. I turned around at once and tried to see through the darkness, but for a moment I was quite blind. I started to grope my way back but had not gone more than a step or two when I was hit, and I went down. I must have been right beside the gong, because after an interval I became vaguely conscious that I was lying under it. My head was hurting, and I felt it, and it seemed to be bleeding. I tried to call out, but I was weak and dizzy, and I could not seem to make a sound. Then I noticed the stick that hangs by the gong and found that I could reach it. I banged out all the tunes that came into my head, and suddenly I was hit again, and I went out like a light. I woke up in bed here."

Richard stirred and asked soberly, "Did you sit up to play the gong?"

"Good lord, no," Berg said. "Remember, I couldn't even call out."

"Then how did you manage to play 'Swanee River'? If you were

lying on the floor, you could not have reached more than two notes—
I tried it."

CHAPTER
30

BERG TOOK OUT a fresh cigarette, and Rosalie bustled to light it. "That's
funny, Dick," he said slowly. "Perhaps I have longer arms than you."

"Let's measure," Richard said promptly, but at that moment the
door opened and Rhynda, Amy and Donald poured into the room.
Amy demanded to know, in a loud voice, why they had been sent
downstairs for questioning and then left to their own devices.

Joe drowned her out. "Sit down here, youse," he said belligerently. "Before anyone leaves this room there's going to be an arrest."

A general gasp went up, and he turned importantly to Rhynda.

"You," he barked. "There was a lot of time last night that you
ain't accounted for. What were you doin'?"

"I was in the bathroom," Rhynda said coldly.

"For over half an hour?"

"Certainly—I was washing out some things. You know perfectly
well that it's almost impossible to get in there in the daytime."

Joe looked a bit balked, and Richard broke in. "Berg," he said,
"were you conscious when you were thrown out of the window?"

"I've told you that I wasn't."

Richard said oddly, "You haven't changed your mind on that
point?"

Berg raised his eyebrows, and there was a moment of silence.
When he spoke, I could have sworn that there was a faint regret in
his voice. "No," he said, "I'll stick to my first story."

"Then why were you dropped out and then carefully moved from
where you landed and laid across the path?"

"Was that done?" Berg asked politely.

"Yes. There were two distinct heelmarks, but no toemarks. Since
you must have landed on your feet, you would certainly have fallen
back towards the house, and since you were unconscious, you would
have remained there. So you must have been moved."

"Strange," murmured Berg.

"Wait a minute!" Joe thundered, and everybody fell silent. Having got to the floor, he scratched his head in evident perplexity as to
his next move. "Wait a minute," he repeated uncertainly, and after a

moment's thought added, "Suppose you let me do the questioning."

"Pleasure," said Richard amiably.

"No use jumpin' around from one thing to another."

"Right," said Richard.

Joe turned back to his audience and fixed a gimlet eye on Amy.

"Now, then, you, Miss Perrin, what was the idea of throwin' them black-headed pins around? Tryin' to put the blame on Mrs. Ballinger?"

"Black-headed pins?" said Amy scornfully. "I never saw one in my life."

"Not one?" Rhynda murmured. "In all the hundreds of corsages you must have received?"

Amy flashed her a malevolent glance and said, "No. They usually send lavender-headed pins with orchids."

Rhynda laughed, and Joe shouted for silence. He produced the pin we had just found in the curtain and waved it under Amy's nose. "Have you ever seen this before?"

Amy drew back her head sharply. "Never," she said, "and I'll thank you to remove it from my face."

Joe swung around on Donald Tait. "You ever see this before?"

"Never met it," said Donald mildly. "Not even a nodding acquaintance."

"You're lyin'," Joe growled.

Amy burst into a flood of talk about how she was going to send for her lawyer, who would undoubtedly reduce Joe to a state where he would wish he had never been born.

Richard was talking to Berg again, quietly. " 'The Elms' is all right—also 'Far Point' or 'Windy Point'—but 'Harrington' shows a certain amount of conceit. If you must have a family name, why not 'Ballinger'? It's better-suited to the place—it's been owned by Ballingers for generations."

Berg laughed shortly. "I don't know what you're talking about, but I don't like your tone. I'm going to get my lawyer down—he can come with Amy's lawyer, and they'll be company for each other."

"I don't like to make a point of it," Richard said, "but you seem to have forgotten that I'm your lawyer. You engaged me last November and brought me along this time so that your lawyer would be handy in case of necessity."

"And instead of protecting me," Berg took him up bitterly, "you stand there asking me insulting questions."

"My father is very sticky about the sort of things we take on," Richard said.

Amy was still shouting, and I sidled closer to Richard so that I would not miss anything. Rhynda moved with me and stayed close beside me.

"The telephone was out on the dining-room table," Richard was saying, "with blood on it, for all to see as the weapon which was used on you, but the cut on your head, which was made with the kitchen knife, was dead straight, not curved at all. You know, the minute I saw that cut I knew it had not been made by the telephone. I wonder why it was not sufficient for you to have been hit only with the telephone?"

"I was cut with a knife?" Berg asked.

"Evidently."

"Ghastly," Berg muttered.

"Well, no, not really. Neither the blow with the telephone, if there was such a blow, nor the cut was very bad."

"I lost a lot of blood, though," Berg said, almost resentfully. "The doctor said so."

"How do you know? Did you hear him say so?"

"No," said Berg. "Aunt Mabel told me."

"Oh. Well, the doctor was mistaken. There wasn't much blood— we looked everywhere for it. There was a bloodstained cloth, and about three extra drops. The cut was very superficial."

Berg sighed and murmured, "Lucky escape, wasn't it?"

"Escape?" Richard repeated and hoisted his eyebrows as high as they would go.

Berg moved restlessly and said after a moment, "You're—not going to tell Joe, are you, Dick?"

"I must. You know that."

"Honor of the Joneses," said Berg wryly. "I should have brought Sam Stephens instead of you. Only I didn't think the old lady would swallow him."

"Nor would she. Sam would never have done—he looks a proper thug."

"I know. That's why I decided on you. But you've done the complete boomerang on me."

Richard shrugged. "Joe would always have been here."

"Yes, and he probably would have hounded Amy to the hot seat, and a very good place for her, too."

I was suddenly conscious that Rhynda was gripping my arm with desperate fingers. I turned to look at her and saw that her head was bent and she was crying quietly.

Joe turned on us at this point and bellowed, "What are youse all talking about? Why can't I have silence while I investigate this thing?"

He was glaring at Richard, but his expression changed to one of blank astonishment as Richard said, "I'm sorry, Joe, but if you wouldn't mind holding up the investigation for a bit, I think Berg wants to confess."

CHAPTER
31

THERE WAS A DEAD silence, and then Mrs. Ballinger gave a little scream.

Berg looked around at us calmly. "No," he said. "Really, there's nothing."

"Wait a minute," Richard broke in. "If you don't want to tell it, suppose you let me? You can correct me when I go wrong."

Berg laughed. "You'll be wrong from start to finish."

"No, I don't think so," Richard said, and half turned to the others. They were nearly all gaping with open mouths, including even Joe. Richard put on a good imitation of a lawyer and cleared his throat.

"Berg came down here about a week before the houseparty and arranged that contraption in the attic. He tried it out and frightened Mrs. Ballinger and Leigh, and then he left. Leigh heard him go."

Berg said, "Where did I go? No trains at that hour."

"You came and went in a car which you had hired that day from the Hamden Auto Hire Company."

"All the details," said Berg, smiling. "Only it happens that I was out with Rhynda on that particular night."

Rhynda covered her face with her hands. "Oh," she groaned, "can't you leave me out of it?"

Richard turned to her. "Did you stay out late that night, Rhynda? Don't lie, because I know about it, anyway."

"No," she sobbed. "I was home by eight o'clock, because I knew John was coming back early."

Richard nodded. "Berg drove straight out here after he had left you. He had a flashlight with him, and he'd planned the thing carefully in his mind."

"Wait a minute," Berg interrupted. "For God's sake, let me tell it. You're making a botch of it."

Richard agreed, and Berg settled himself more comfortably and smoothed back his hair.

"It all began when I fell in love with Rhynda."

Rhynda muttered, "Oh, Berg!" and moved closer to me. I put my arm around her.

"I wanted her," Berg continued, "but I knew that it wasn't possible unless I had a decent income and a nice place to live. Rhynda always liked nice things. I knew I couldn't earn an adequate income. Nobody seemed to want my services, and if they did put up with me, they never paid me anything.

"It occurred to me that if John were to die accidentally, his insurance would make a handsome sum for Rhynda—he carried double indemnity. Not only that, but Freda and I would then split his share of our trust fund. Further, if Freda were to die, I would get the entire amount from the fund, something like two hundred and twenty-five dollars a month that could be depended upon. With that and Rhynda's insurance, and perhaps a job for the sake of appearances and cigarette money, I thought we could manage.

"I'd heard about Aunt Mabel's angina and knew that the house was to be left to John, Freda and myself."

Amy raised her head sharply and started to interrupt, but Berg got in ahead of her. "It's all right, Greedy," he said smoothly. "We were to get the house because we had the Ballinger name. You were to be compensated, but just how I don't know and don't care." Amy subsided, and he resumed. "I thought it would make a nice country gentleman sort of place for us. Rhynda could raise all the dogs for show that she wanted, and we might even have horses.

"I figured that the idea was a good one, but if I was to get the house John and Freda must be disposed of before the angina got Aunt Mabel, because the house was not like the trust fund. There would be no reversion to me, and the chances were that it would simply be sold and the money divided. So I decided to do it all in a hurry, and I arranged it for the Christmas holiday."

He paused to get another cigarette, but this time Rosalie made no move to light it for him. I observed, with a little thrill of horror, that he was enjoying himself thoroughly.

"I wanted the deaths to appear accidental, and in deference to Aunt Mabel's superstitious beliefs, I decided to play up the old ghost story. I thought it might make the accidents more reasonable—nervous excitement, you know—and I hoped that the horror and fear would finish Aunt Mabel."

Mrs. Ballinger started to thunder, "I haven't got angina—" but was peremptorily silenced by Joe.

Berg, after an annoyed frown at the interruption, took up the tale again. "As Dick said, I fixed the brick in the attic that night, and I fixed John's scaffolding, too—I found it lying up there. After that I got a tasty little supper, taking care not to run into any of you women.

"I could not resist trying out my apparatus on you. I was lucky with it, too. I found I had to have wind to work it properly, and there was nearly always wind.

"I brought Dick to the houseparty so that he would pay some attention to Rhynda. I knew they'd get on well enough together, and I did not want anyone to think that I was interested in her. I wanted her to be occupied, too, so that she would not catch on to what I was doing. But you did catch on, didn't you, Rhynda?"

Rhynda, staring at the floor with dropped head, made no reply.

"I waited all day for John's accident," Berg resumed, "but he did not use the scaffold until late in the afternoon. When he did, it broke pretty promptly, and that part of it was done.

"Leigh helped me tremendously there by telling me to take the scaffold away. I took it down to the cellar and was looking around for a good hiding place, when Doris came down for something, so I had to throw it under the stairs.

"I came back as soon as I could and hid it, but the harm had already been done.

"I was determined to carry it through, though, with all the ghostly embellishments, so I got up that night and moved John to the chair, and Freda saw me. I did not know about Freda until Leigh told Dick and me at our little conference. Fortunately, Freda had not named me.

"I told Leigh to pump her, and I went off myself to find her and somehow shut her up forever. I never liked her, anyway. She loaned me ten dollars once and never ceased to dun me for it thereafter. And I have rarely seen a more unattractive woman."

Richard murmured, "Never mind the personalities," and even Joe muttered gruffly, "For Chrissake, get on with it."

Berg ignored them and continued to enjoy his position in the spotlight.

"I was a bit disturbed to find that Freda was missing and that everyone was searching for her. She was found by dinner time, and after dinner I could not get her alone. After she went upstairs with Leigh I played hide-and-seek in their two bedrooms and in the hall, listening to as much of their conversation as possible, so that I could interrupt at once if Freda started getting too confidential.

"At last I heard Freda say that she was going to the bathroom, so I hurried there before her and hid in the closet. I dropped that black-headed pin there. I'd picked it up in Aunt Mabel's room and had decided that a few clues leading elsewhere would do not harm just in case Freda's death would not be considered accidental.

"When it was found—and all the sleuths seemed to regard it as a valuable clue—I deliberately put the others around in the various significant places. Even the one in Amy's room—I put that in this morning." He stopped to laugh reminiscently. "I was supposed to be in the bathroom, and Aunt Mabel and Rosalie Nightingale there were too modest to see me go and come.

"But about Freda. She came into the bathroom alone, but she was still talking, and I realized that Leigh must be outside. I knew there was no time to be lost, so I picked up the hammer that was so conveniently there, slid out of the closet quietly, and hit her as she leaned over the basin and turned on the faucet. Fortunately she had her back to me, and she never made a sound. I caught her so that Leigh would not hear her fall and immediately turned on the water in the bathtub. I undressed her and got her in.

"I had not intended to move Freda's body. I thought it would be of no particular use and was too dangerous. But when Leigh went down for her supper I couldn't resist doing it—it was so easy, and the effect so dramatic." He laughed again, into the stunned silence of the room. "I was glad I'd done it afterwards, because I thought it might create an impression that the attack was directed at all the Ballingers.

"I had intended to attack myself tonight instead of last night, but I had gone downstairs with the telephone to put it in a handy place and make my plans when I heard someone come out of Rhynda's room. I thought it was Leigh, and I felt sure that she was coming down—in fact, she came straight for the top of the stairs. I hit my forehead as hard as I could with the telephone, and then I heard her walk away from the stairs. I went halfway up and heard her go to the bathroom. I figured that it might still be all right—she might have decided to go to the bathroom before coming down.

"I looked around for a convenient place to lie down, but I was a bit uneasy about my wound; it wasn't hurting enough. I went to the dining room, put the telephone down on the table, switched on the light, and looked at myself in the mirror, and I have never seen a more innocuous looking wound in my life. I had to work fast then. I picked up a cloth from a side table, went to the kitchen and got a knife, came back to the dining room, and made a cut straight through the bruise that was already on my forehead. I bloodied the telephone a bit, wiped it clean of fingerprints, and returned it to the table. I turned off the light and made my way in the dark, to the front hall. I still had the knife, so I wiped it off and put it into Rhynda's coat pocket in the closet.

"I waited anxiously then for Leigh to come down, but there was no sound. I mopped at the blood with the cloth and realized that I was beginning to feel faint, and I got a bit desperate. I went to the gong and played it, but absolutely no one paid any attention. I had about decided to take myself and the weapon upstairs and make some sort of noise up there, when I heard Leigh come out again. I know that door because it has a little squeak. But I had no way of knowing that it was Rhynda who had come out the first time, or that she was, even then, sitting in my room, waiting to talk to me.

"This time it really was Leigh, but I took no chances. I went and played the gong again and dropped one of the black-headed pins onto the floor beneath it. I had two with me.

"I should have dropped myself onto the floor beside the pin, but I made the mistake of going back to the stairs to see if Leigh was coming. I could not see or hear anything until suddenly there she was, almost upon me. I managed to step aside silently and slipped into the music room, and the next instant she had the hall light on.

"I heard her go around into the back hall and then on into the kitchen. I did not quite know what to do then. I was feeling dizzy and faint, and I thoughtlessly switched off the hall light—another mistake, I suppose.

"I waited at the foot of the stairs for what seemed hours, but at last I heard her open the door to the back hall. Then she closed it again, went into the dining room, and retreated once more." He glanced at me and added, "I hate an indecisive woman."

I opened my mouth to retort, but Joe shut me up.

Berg resumed. "While I was wondering what her next antic would be, she suddenly came rushing through from the back hall, and before I could lie down at the foot of the stairs, she stopped dead, and I realized that somehow she could see me.

"At that moment, Rhynda called from the top of the stairs, and I made an involuntary, forward movement. It finished Smith—she was off like a scared rabbit and went flying out the front door.

"I think I ran even faster than she did. I got into that front room and was lucky to find that the window was not locked and didn't stick. I vaulted over the sill and landed in the flowerbed, making the now-famous heelmarks. I threw the blood-soaked cloth over the shrubbery and closed my hand tightly on the remaining pin.

"Either it was very dark or Leigh was blind and deaf with hysteria, for it was not a second later that she stumbled over me. I went out like a light, then, in peace and comfort."

We all stared at him in silence as he finished his extraordinary recital with evident pleasure in himself and his delivery.

CHAPTER
32

THE SHOCKED SILENCE was broken by Mrs. Ballinger, who had hysterics. Amy fought with Rosalie Hannahs to minister to her, and I figured that Amy had a bigger eye than ever now, on the main chance. Rosalie too, was evidently beginning to think that there might be something in it for her.

"What did she mean when she said she didn't have angina?" I asked of nobody in particular.

Berg laughed. "I've suspected for several days now that the old pest didn't have it after all. I heard her telling Rosalie about it. It's never been diagnosed, except by herself. She read it up in a medical book and decided that she had all the symptoms, but she would not go to a doctor because of the expense. That thing she wears around her neck is merely a small bottle of smelling salts."

"But what about her attacks?"

"Nobody has ever seen her have one. She described them to us and made them sound ghastly, but she would not tell you or Doris about them because she was afraid you might demand more wages if you knew you were attending an invalid. I believe she broke down the other day and let O'Beirne examine her, and he laughed her angina out of existence. Would have been a good joke on me—I'd have had to arrange another accident."

Richard and I stared at him, and Richard asked, with a sort of cold curiosity, "Don't you take this thing seriously at all?"

"Seriously?" Berg laughed. "No. It means a few years in a loony bin, and then I'll write a book about it."

"Claiming insanity?"

"Naturally. It must be obvious to you that I am mentally unbalanced—whatever. Listen, Dick, will you phone Sam Stephens for me?"

Richard nodded, and, putting his arm through mine, marched me out of the room. Rhynda trailed after us, leaving Berg, Joe and Donald Tait to each other. As the door closed I heard Joe say happily, "Outa that bed, brother, and get yourself dressed—and no lavender pants, either, see? They wouldn't match the inside of our jail."

Rhynda caught up with us and laid a hand on my arm. "Wait a minute. I have to say my little piece. I'm sorry that I had to be so lacking in finesse, but I was honestly frightened half out of my wits. I knew Berg was up to something, and when John and Freda died I began to have a vague idea of what it was, but I had no proof of any sort—nothing. I wanted no connection with Berg of any sort, and I tried to connect up with Richard instead. I thought it might work because John had started to be jealous at my going about with other men, and at the Christmas Eve party he backed me into a corner and told me off properly about flirting with Richard. It was the first time he had done that, and I was furious. I guess that's why I was so rude to you that night, Leigh. Later on, when I claimed Richard, it was funny to see your face."

"Rubbish!" I said shortly.

Rhynda laughed, almost happily. "Well, I'm off to pack. And if I ever come out to the country again, you can have me certified."

She walked off, humming, and I said, "Now she's all cheered up again. I wonder what it's like always to be either bubbling over or down in the dumps."

"I hope you're feeling cheery enough yourself to accept me,

should I happen to propose to you," he said mildly.

"Absolutely. Go ahead."

"No," he said. "I'd better think it over first. And anyway, I have to phone Sam."

I followed him downstairs. "Is Berg really going to get off as lightly as he thinks?"

"No, he's not. He always was unduly optimistic. But I'm not crying about it, Smithy. He deserves whatever he gets."

He put his hand on the telephone, and I said, "Wait a minute. You read me out that list of queer things that I found in the various bedrooms, and your false teeth, my Elsie books, and Berg's list of names for the house have all been explained, but I still don't understand Amy's maternity dress, Donald Tait's stink bombs, Mrs. Ballinger's prospectus for a boys' school, or Rosalie's unused ticket for Elkton."

He grinned at me. "They have no bearing on the matter, but I suppose I'll have to explain. Joe was right—you ain't called Nosey Smith for nothin'.

"Rosalie's ticket pretty nearly speaks for itself. She describes it as a tragedy and says she was to buy her ticket and meet dear Martin at the station. They were eloping, for no very good reason, but Martin never showed up. She keeps the ticket for sentimental reasons and is dedicating the rest of her life to a search for him.

"Amy readily explained that the stink bombs and the maternity gown were routine equipment when she and Donald went to weekend parties. It seems you can have no end of a good time with the stink bombs, and the gown is Donald's fancy dress costume.

"That catalogue from the boys' school that you found in Mrs. Ballinger's room is giving Amy a lot of headaches. It seems the old lady is thinking of adopting a boy from a local orphanage. The place is one of her charities, and she heard that the kid is a wizard carpenter—seems to be born to it. Her idea is to give him a gentlemen's education at the cheapest boarding school she can find, and thus gain the awe and admiration of the village and the respect of the orphanage. She said she wanted a man around the place in her old age, but I think the main idea is that, as time goes on, the kid can do all the repair work, free of charge. It's killing two birds with one stone, you see—she loves applause, and she loves to save money."

The front doorbell rang stridently, and after a moment Doris appeared from the back hall. She opened the door and was engaged for some time in what seemed to be a heated discussion. Presently she looked over her shoulder and called to Richard, "There's three men here, come about the murders. I keep telling them Joe's seeing to it, but they won't listen."

"You'll have to let them go up," Richard said gravely. "Can't interfere with the law."

Doris stood back, looking aggrieved, and as the three men came in I directed them upstairs. Richard looked after them as they clattered off and said softly, "Just too late, you interfering louses. This is Joe's day."

He got his connection in New York then, and I explained about Berg to Doris, who was standing with her mouth hanging open. When I had finished, she refused point-blank to believe any of it. Berg had always been her favorite, and she was quite certain that he was shielding someone, probably Amy. She went off, muttering to herself.

Richard hung up the receiver and stood up.

"Sam coming?" I asked.

"Yes. Look here, Smithy, I've decided to propose to you."

"Have you thought it over?"

"Yes."

I scuffed around a bit and said, "What made you finally decide?"

"Oh well. I might go farther and do worse, you know, and it's time I settled down."

"All right," I said cheerfully. "I accept. I don't know about settling down, or doing worse, but I do need five meals a day."

THE END

A catalog of Rue Morgue Press titles as of December 1999

The Black Gloves by Constance & Gwenyth Little. "I'm relishing every madcap moment."—*Murder Most Cozy*. Welcome to the Vickers estate near East Orange, New Jersey, where the middle class is destroying the neighborhood, erecting their horrid little cottages, playing on the Vickers tennis court, and generally disrupting the comfortable life of Hammond Vickers no end. It's bad enough that he had to shell out good money to his daughter Lissa a Reno divorce only to have her brute of an es-husband show up on his doorstep. But why does there also have to be a corpse in the cellar? And lights going on and off in the attic? First published in 1939.   **0-915230-20-8 $14.00**

The Black Honeymoon by Constance & Gwenyth Little. Can you murder someone with feathers? If you don't believe feathers are lethal, then you probably haven't read a Little mystery. No, Uncle Richard wasn't tickled to death—though we can't make the same guarantee for readers—but the hyper-allergic rich man did manage to sneeze himself into the hereafter in his hospital room. Suspicion falls on his nurse, young Miriel Mason, who recently married the dead man's nephew, an army officer on furlough. To clear herself of murder as well as charges of being a gold-digger, Miriel summons private detective Kelly, an old crony of her father's, who gets himself hired as a servant even though he can't cook, clean or serve. First published in 1944.   **0-915230-21-6 $14.00**

Great Black Kanba by Constance & Gwenyth Little. "If you love train mysteries as much as I do, hop on the Trans-Australia Railway in *Great Black Kanba*, a fast and funny 1944 novel by the talented (Littles)."—Jon L. Breen, *Ellery Queen's Mystery Magazine*. "I have decided to add *Kanba* to my favorite mysteries of all time list!...a zany ride I'll definitely take again and again."—Diane Plumley in the Murder Ink newsletter. When a young American woman wakes up on an Australia train with a bump on her head and no memory, she suddenly finds out that she's engaged to two different men and the chief suspect in a murder case. But she's almost more upset to discover that she appears to have absolutely dreadful taste in clothing. It all adds up to some delightful mischief—call it Cornell Woolrich on laughing gas.   **0-915230-22-4 $14.00**

The Grey Mist Murders by Constance & Gwenyth Little. Who—or what—is the mysterious figure that emerges from the grey mist to strike down several passengers on the final leg of a round-the-world sea voyage? Is it the same shadowy entity that persists in leaving three matches outside Lady Marsh's cabin every morning? And why does one flimsy negligee seem to pop up at every turn? When Carla Bray first heard things go bump in the night, she hardly expected to find a corpse in the adjoining cabin. Nor did she expect to find herself the chief suspect in the murders. Robert Arnold, a sardonic young man who joined the ship in Tahiti, makes a play for Carla but if he's really interested in helping to clear her of murder, why does he spend so much time courting other women on board? This 1938 effort was the Littles' first book.   **0-915230-26-7 $14.00**

Murder is a Collector's Item by Elizabeth Dean. "(It) froths over with the same effervescent humor as the best Hepburn-Grant films."—Sujata Massey. "Completely enjoyable."—*New York Times.* "Fast and funny."—*The New Yorker.* Twenty-six-year-old Emma Marsh isn't much at spelling or geography and perhaps she butchers the odd literary quotation or two, but she's a keen judge of character and more than able to hold her own when it comes to selling antiques or solving murders. When she stumbles upon the body of a rich collector on the floor of the Boston antiques shop where she works, suspicion quickly falls upon her missing boss. Emma knows Jeff Graham is no murderer, but veteran homicide copy Jerry Donovan doesn't share her convictions, and Emma enlists the aid of Hank Fairbanks, her wealthy boyfriend and would-be criminologist, to nab the real killer. Originally published in 1939, *Murder is a Collector's Item* was the first of three books featuring Emma. Smoothly written and sparkling with dry, sophisticated humor, this nearly forgotten milestone combines an intriguing puzzle with an entertaining portrait of a self-possessed young woman on her own in Boston toward the end of the Great Depression. **0-915230-19-4 $14.00**

Murder is a Serious Business by Elizabeth Dean. It's 1940 and the Thirsty Thirties are over but you couldn't tell it by the gang at J. Graham Antiques where clerk Emma Marsh, her would-be criminologist boyfriend Hank, and boss Jeff Graham trade barbs in between shots of scotch when they aren't bothered by the rare customer. Trouble starts when Emma and crew head for a weekend at Amos Currier's country estate to inventory the man's antiques collection. It isn't long before the bodies start falling and once again Emma is forced to turn sleuth in order to prove that her boss isn't a killer. Emma is sure there's a good reason why Jeff didn't mention that he had Amos' 18th century silver muffineer hidden in his desk drawer back at the shop. Filled with the same clever dialog and eccentric characters that made *Murder is a Collector's Item* an absolute delight, this second Emma Marsh novel offers up an unusual approach to crime solving as well as a sidesplitting look at the peculiar world of antiques. **0-915230-28-3 $14.95**

Murder, Chop Chop by James Norman. "The book has the butter-wouldn't-melt-in-his-mouth cool of Rick in *Casablanca.*"—*The Rocky Mountain News.* "Amuses the reader no end."—*Mystery News.* "This long out-of-print masterpiece is intricately plotted, full of eccentric characters and very humorous indeed. Highly recommended."—*Mysteries by Mail.* Meet Gimiendo Hernandez Quinto, a gigantic Mexican who once rode with Pancho Villa and who now trains *guerrilleros* for the Nationalist Chinese government when he isn't solving murders. At his side is a beautiful Eurasian known as Mountain of Virtue, a woman as dangerous to men as she is irresistible. Then there's Mildred Woodford, a hard-drinking British journalist; John Tate, a portly American calligrapher who wasn't made for adventure; Lieutenant Chi, a young Hunanese patriot weighted down with the cares of China and the Brooklyn Dodgers; and a host of others, anyone of whom may have killed Abe Harrow, an ambulance driver who appears to have died at three different times. There's also a cipher or two to crack, a train with a mind of its own, and Chiang Kai-shek's false teeth, which have gone mysteriously missing. First published in 1942. **0-915230-16-X $13.00**

Death at The Dog by Joanna Cannan. "Worthy of being discussed in the same breath with an Agatha Christie or Josephine Tey...anyone who enjoys Golden Age mysteries will surely enjoy this one."—Sally Fellows, *Mystery News*. "Skilled writing and brilliant characterization."—*Times of London*. "An excellent English rural tale."—Jacques Barzun & Wendell Hertig Taylor in *A Catalogue of Crime*. Set in late 1939 during the first anxious months of World War II, *Death at The Dog*, which was first published in 1941, is a wonderful example of the classic English detective novel that first flourished between the two World Wars. Set in a picturesque village filled with thatched-roof-cottages, eccentric villagers and genial pubs, it's as well-plotted as a Christie, with clues abundantly and fairly planted, and as deftly written as the best of the books by either Sayers or Marsh, filled with quotable lines and perceptive observations on the human condition. Cannan had a gift for characterization that's second to none in Golden Age detective fiction, and she created two memorable lead characters. One of them is Inspector Guy Northeast, a lonely young Scotland Yard inspector who makes his second and final appearance here and finds himself hopelessly smitten with the chief suspect in the murder of a village tyrant. The other is the "lady novelist" Crescy Hardwick, an unconventional and ultimately unobtainable woman a number of years guy's senior, who is able to pierce his armor and see the unhappiness that haunts the detective's private moments. Well aware that all the evidence seems to point to her, she is also able—unlike her less imaginative fellow villagers—to see how very good Northeast is at his job.   **0-915230-23-2 $14.00**

They Rang Up the Police by Joanna Cannan. When Delia Cathcart and Major Willoughby disappear from their quiet English village one Saturday morning in July 1937, it looks like a simple case of a frustrated spinster running off for a bit of fun with a straying husband. But as the hours turn into days, Inspector Guy Northeast begins to suspect that she may have been the victim of foul play. On the surface, Delia appeared to be a quite ordinary middle-aged Englishwoman content to spend her evenings with her sisters and her days with her beloved horses. But Delia led a secret life—and Guy turns up more than one person who would like to see Delia dead. Except Delia wasn't the only person with a secret...Never published in the United States, *They Rang Up the Police* appeared in England in 1939.   **0-915230-27-5 $14.00**

Cook Up a Crime by Charlotte Murray Russell. "Perhaps the mother of today's "cozy" mystery...amateur sleuth Jane has a personality guaranteed to entertain the most demanding reader."—Andy Plonka, *The Mystery Reader*. "Some wonderful old time recipes...highly recommended."—*Mysteries by Mail*. Meet Jane Amanda Edwards, a self-styled "full-fashioned" spinster who complains she hasn't looked at herself in a full-length mirror since Helen Hokinson started drawing for *The New Yorker*. But you can always count on Jane to look into other people's affairs, especially when there's a juicy murder case to investigate. In this 1951 title Jane goes searching for recipes (included between chapters) for a cookbook project and finds a body instead. And once again her lily-of-the-field brother Arthur goes looking for love, finds strong drink, and is eventually discovered clutching the murder weapon.   **0-915230-18-6 $13.00**

The Man from Tibet by Clyde B. Clason. Locked inside the Tibetan Room of his Chicago luxury apartment, the rich antiquarian was overheard repeating a forbidden occult chant under the watchful eyes of Buddhist gods. When the doors were opened it appeared that he had succumbed to a heart attack. But the elderly Roman historian and sometime amateur sleuth Theocritus Lucius Westborough is convinced that Adam Merriweather's death was anything but natural and that the weapon was an eighth century Tibetan manuscript. It it's murder, who could have done it, and how? Suspects abound. There's's Tsongpun Bonbo, the gentle Tibetan lama from whom the manuscript was originally stolen; Chang, Merriweather's scholarly Tibetan secretary who had fled a Himalayan monastery; Merriweather's son Vincent, who disliked his father and stood to inherit a fortune; Dr. Jed Merriweather, the dead man's brother, who came to Chicago to beg for funds to continue his archaeological digs in Asia; Dr. Walters, the dead man's physician, who guarded a secret; and Janice Shelton, his young ward, who found herself being pushed by Merriweather into marrying his son. How the murder was accomplished has earned praise from such impossible crime connoisseurs as Robert C.S. Adey, who cited Clason's "highly original and practical locked-room murder method."　　　　　　　　　　**0-915230-17-8　$14.00**

The Mirror by Marlys Millhiser. "Completely enjoyable."—*Library Journal* . "A great deal of fun."—*Publishers Weekly*. How could you not be intrigued, as one reviewer pointed out, by a novel in which "you find the main character marrying her own grandfather and giving birth to her own mother?" Such is the situation in Marlys Millhiser's classic novel (a Mystery Guild selection originally published by Putnam in 1978) of two women who end up living each other's lives after they look into an antique Chinese mirror. Twenty-year-old Shay Garrett is not aware that she's pregnant and is having second thoughts about marrying Marek Weir when she's suddenly transported back 78 years in time into the body of Brandy McCabe, her own grandmother, who is unwillingly about to be married off to miner Corbin Strock. Shay's in shock but she still recognizes that the picture of her grandfather that hangs in the family home doesn't resemble her husband-to-be. But marry Corbin she does and off she goes to the high mining town of Nederland, where this thoroughly modern young woman has to learn to cope with such things as wood cooking stoves and—to her—old-fashioned attitudes about sex. In the meantime, Brandy McCabe is finding it even harder to cope with life in the Boulder, Co., of 1978.　　　　　　**0-915230-15-1　$14.95**

About The Rue Morgue Press

The Rue Morgue Press vintage mystery line is designed to bring back into print those books that were favorites of readers between the turn of the century and the 1960s. The editors welcome suggestions for reprints. To receive our catalog or make suggestions, write The Rue Morgue Press, P.O. Box 4119, Boulder, Colorado 80306.